Mother Blue &
The Deep Down Under

Also By Ellen Orleans

Inside, The World Is Orange

Outreach

The Inflatable Butch

Still Can't Keep A Straight Face

The Butches of Madison County

Who Cares If It's A Choice?

Can't Keep A Straight Face

Boulder Voices: Lesbian, Gay and Bisexual Citizens of Boulder County Tell Their Stories; Editor

Mother Blue &
The Deep Down Under

Stories Inspired by Caribou Ranch Open Space

Ellen Orleans

The story "The Cook's Son," appeared in Volume 43, Issue 1
of *Pilgrimage Magazine,* Colorado State University at Pueblo.

For information, contact:
Ellen Orleans, Sensible Shoes Press
P.O. Box 1348; Boulder, Colorado 80306

Cover photo by Ellen Orleans
Author photos by Martha Coder and Magic Morningstar
Book design by HR Hegnauer

First printing, 2020
Second printing, 2023

10 9 8 7 6 5 4 3 2 1

For the
souls and spirits
of Caribou—
may you roam free.

Bunkhouse where Alma,
Edward and Ohio Bill lived

Blue Bird Mine

Edward's
Hidden Coins

Aspen
Grove

Switzerland Trail Railroad Tracks

Where
Ruth drew

Sama's
Pasture

DeLonde
Homestead

Where the
writer wrote

Blue Bird Loop

DeLonde Creek

Beaver
Pond

Where the Ranger hiked

Where Annie Ames
Archer hiked

Flower
Meadow

DeLonde
Trail ⟶

CARIBOU
RANCH
OPEN
SPACE

North Boulder
Creek

where Edward sat
among the aspens

BOULDER COUNTY,
COLORADO

Where Russell and Bow
stood and listened

Contents

Introduction

NORTHWEST OF NEDERLAND, Colorado, off the Peak-to-Peak Highway, Boulder County's Caribou Ranch Open Space has been home to hunting grounds, a silver mine, a recording studio, a horse ranch, a Hollywood movie set, train tracks for the Switzerland Trail railroad, and more recently, trails for hikers, snowshoers, and nature enthusiasts.

In 2015, I was awarded an artist's residency at this remarkable place. For six days in mid-July, I immersed myself in reading, writing, walking, wildlife watching, riverbank sitting, moon gazing, and extreme wildflower awe. Against this backdrop, I began imagining the lives of those who had visited Caribou before me.

In my application for the residency, I had proposed writing a series of "micro" stories inspired by the people of Caribou. However, as often happens in writing, my characters shook their fictional heads and demanded more depth and details. They wanted their own back stories and complex motivations. The proposed micro stories blossomed in length and intricacy.

While the settings are real, the characters in these stories spring from my imagination. Instead of being tied to known historical facts (which, in themselves, were often sketchy), I let my artistic license run amuck, taking joy in giving voice to those who might have been.

Take a walk at Caribou. Perhaps you'll hear them too.

The Storyteller

THIS IS OUR summer home, these mountains, this valley, this cold-running creek where the red willows make their home.

My mother selects and cuts. We children bundle. My auntie walks between us, delivering the branches. The third time, she begins, "A long time ago, a black-tipped hawk, high in a tall dead tree, spied three field mice at the edge of the meadow. When the hawk swooped..."

"Wasn't it a fox who saw the mice?" my older sister asks. "That's what Uncle told us—"

"No, it's a fire," my cousin interrupts, "and a whole field of mice are running—"

My auntie quiets us. "When the hawk swooped, one mouse caught the shift of light. The nimble creature darted, other mice followed, all scampering through the cocoon grass, around the edge of a speckled rock, and up the rough bark of the green-fingered tree. There, they hid in the safety of its cones."

"Today, when you look closely at that tree's shaggy cone"—here Auntie unfolds her palm—"you can still see the mouse's legs and tail poking out."

My sister draws close, touching the cone's feathery "tail" and "legs." I stop my bundling and ask, "How many field mice ran to the tree?"

"Many mice."

"And the hawk never saw them there?"

"Never. They were clever."

I picture a tree full of mice. "While they were inside the cones, what did the mice do? While its cones were hiding the mice, what did the tree do?"

My auntie laughs. "That's easy. They told each other stories."

The Cook's Son

1877

MY FATHER USED to be the cook, but now my mother is, on account of my father being gone away. Cooking for wrecked, hungry men is terrible hard work, but my mother says she can do it and she does.

"Beggars can't be choosers," says Mr. Otis Farnley, the pay man with twisty mustache who is in charge of the miners at Blue Bird.

"We're not beggars, Edward," Ma tells me, her two arms carrying the tub of dirty wash water out back for dumping. "I'm only cooking 'til your Pa comes back."

I know Pa ain't coming back. *Isn't* coming back. Ma says just cause I'm a little slow doesn't mean I can't learn to speak right. Speaking words isn't my best thing, but I'm a good counter. Numbers. Money. Putting things in order. I'm very good at that.

Like this row of pine cones. I can align them up, smallest to biggest. Skinny to round. Rocks, too.

Smoothest to roughest. Shiny to dull. *Dull. Dullard.* That's what Otis Farnley calls me. Mr. Farnley looks at my lines of rocks and cones and says my brain has holes. My mother says to pay him no attention and to remember Mr. Farnley is only pay man, not Head Man. Head Man is tough but has a kind streak, Ma says.

"Streaks like the blue silver in the rocks the men bring out from the deep down under?"

"Yes," Ma says, "Streaks run through people too."

Head Man says children should not live at a mine and should be in school. But I can't hardly read, so school would not be for me. The alignment of letters into words is false to my thinking. I want to home-up letters in words—same letters together or same shape letters together—stick shape, slant shape, round shapes. My name, EDWARD, I want to align it in the order it shows in the alphabet—ADDERW—or by slant, stick, and rounds: AW E DD R . Hard to know where the R, slant and round in one, fits in.

Ma says reading don't work that way, but that's how my brain-with-holes sees it. The letters hopping over and slipping under each other, aligning like the miners do, marching into the down below.

Ma shake-smiles her head when I explain my letters to her. Some days, she calls me ADDER, dropping the W to the ground. ADDER because of the order of the alphabet, because of my way with numbers. I do not tell her that ADDER is also a snake. Snakes are fine by me but Ma does not possess a fondness for them.

ADDER. Everyone needs a nickname, Ma told me that first time, then kissed me on my head. Her words must be true, because the men of the mine have names not their Christian ones. Big Clyde. Skinny Nat. Johnny Crooked Leg, an Italian who's been at Blue Bird for years. Sturdy Joe, who is Cheyenne, and knows all the plants here. Straw-haired Ohio Bill who reads to me from the newspaper and sometimes the Bible, if I ask.

Even though Head Man says children shouldn't be at the mine, Ma is a good cook, original with what she has, which is dried beans and salt pork and cans and cans of vegetables, and, some days, real vegetables that need cut up. When we are lucky, the meat of a deer. So, Head Man says Ma and me can stay.

I wash the men's lunch buckets and bring coal from the pile. I relocate water from the creek to the kitchen. I wash pots and collect wood for when the coal runs low, arranging the sticks thinnest thin thick thicker before feeding them to the cookstove. After supper, I throw empty cans into the rubbish heap by the ravine. I cost Head Man nothing but a little food.

I leave my collections on boulders and fence posts and the edge of the ground so the men in the mines can see the things they miss all day in the down below. Once, when Mr. Farnley wasn't paying attention—and Ma says we should always pay attention—Mr. Farnley tripped over a row of snow balls (rolled in a little grit, some grit, a lot of grit) even though they were on the

5

edge of the ground. He called me a thick-headed oaf, destined for nothing. Mr. Farnley is good with words.

Nights when the men play card games, sometimes I watch. Red diamonds. Black hearts with stems. Red hearts without. Black clovers that should be green by my way of thinking. Numbers go round and round. I don't know why some alignments cause glad hollers and others bring curses, but I know which ones do. Johnny tells me about rules and how rules decide what is hollered at and what is cursed at, but these rules are not steady. I cannot count on them. My rules, I can. Thin cuts cook faster. Thick sticks burn longer.

When Otis Farnley circles up at the table, he tosses me out. When Ma catches me watching, she does too, saying gambling is the Devil's joy.

I like best to align things I can touch, but I also listen to birds, even skip-along bluebirds, for bluebirds are real and not just the name of our mine. I cannot row up sounds, not like rock or twig or carrot rows, but I can sit sounds right in my head. Long calls. Short calls. Crackly and low. Pretty as a song. Angel's joy.

I've been here three summers now and as soon as the snow melts, flowers start. Flowers could be aligned, white to pink to red, lavender to blue to violet, but flowers are for girls so I let them be. There's plenty else to align. Bark fallen from trees, roughest to smoothest, brown to grey to white. Or lichen, six kinds.

"Look at all your pretty mossies," says Johnny. His beard is scraggly like my pale green lichen.

"They are not moss," I tell him politely. "They are lichen and they are gray green, white green, yellow green, and orange."

"That so?" he says and the next day he brings me ore rocks from the mine to align. Large to small. Roughest to rounded. Most blue streaks to least. I keep them for three days. Then Johnny sets them on the wagon that brings them to town to be turned into silver. Goodbye rocks.

A man on a trotting horse draws up to Blue Bird. His black hair and beard are fussy-trimmed, as Big Clyde calls it. (Big Clyde's beard is not trimmed, but grows wild on his ruddy face.) The man sees my lichen aligned in their tin cans on the bunkhouse porch. He tells me that lichen are two plants, algae and fungus, working together, like Ma and me work together. The man is a teacher and says he will swap me a fifty-cent piece for my samples. So now I have money and now I know something new.

When Ma is cooking and I am too much underfoot, putting too many things in rows—soup ladles, cutting knives, drinking cups (most dented to least dented, most chipped to least)—she says, "Adder, go on and sit with the aspen trees."

Aspen trees have limbs. I have limbs. Aspen trees have eyes in their bark. I have eyes in my head. I watch them. They watch me. They watch over me. It is good to sit in the grove.

As I said to you in the beforehand, I am good at watching. This I have been watching for a long time: Otis Farnley cheating the miners. On pay days, I watch him keep small parts of the money, always with a something-to-say about it. *The new men always get less at the start. Complain and we'll find someone else. I paid you extra last week, did you forget?*

Mr. Farnley's excuses turn into stories. *This is because you are not working as speedy as the rest. Now the boss, he don't want to keep you but I said you'd get faster. Don't you tell anyone I helped you.* Worst of all was the time he kept bonuses meant to raise the spirits of the miners. Behind the juniper bush, I listen as I line up pine cones: prettiest to plainest. Strongest to most broken.

At night, after pay days, Otis Farnley buries money. He uses always the same three holes. By the Ponderosa with the bent arm. Next to the spotted rock on the slanted land. Between the tailings pile and stone wall. He drinks liquor before he buries money, so it is double easy to watch him. I make no noise even though he is not a good listener.

On a steamy-kitchen afternoon, Ma drops a full-dinner cook pot on her foot. The pot is slippery from slopped soup and had one handle half broke, so it was not her fault. Otis Farnley was obliged to fix the handle and he had not.

We are lucky because Head Man is there and he takes Ma into town to see a doctor who sets her small bones. When Ma comes back the next day, she works sitting down. She uses a cane. She needs to rest more, so I aim to work more. I cut potatoes and onions and do not align them outright because this tarries supper. Instead, I make the potatoes move in my imaginings. I do the same with carrot rounds and the meat squares. I work quiet and able. I remember to make my knife sharp.

I help, but the food still comes slower. Head Man says it is okay. Otis Farnley says we should hire a new cook, his cousin who works a stove in Georgetown. Head Man says no. Head Man says he can get Nedda the washer woman to help if help is needed.

Otis Farnley false-limps to Ma, whispers. "Bad foot makes you a beggar now, Alma. Beggars can't be choosers. Beggars gotta be..." He lays his hand on her, so I stride directly, carrying the fish knife and whetstone. "Ma," I say, "is this knife sharp enough?"

Otis Farnley moves away.

The next week, I work faster, cooking, hauling, scrubbing, sweeping. I have the men's lunch buckets ready before they awake. Even though I am tired, I sweep the grit into three piles: one big, one small, one in-between. Then I sweep it into one pile and carry it to the ravine. Johnny Crooked Leg and Otis Farnley sit outside, chewing tobacco. Johnny says soon maybe I will be the new cook. Mr. Farnley assembles a sneering face.

After supper, he tries to touch Ma again, but Sturdy Joe and Ohio Bill see, walk to the stove where she is, pretending they need a drinking cup. Otis Farnley leaves off.

Before sleep, as Ma unwinds her long hair from her head, she says does not know if we can stay here. Even with my help and Nedda's help, the food is late to the men. She needs to rest her foot much longer, the doctor has said, if she don't, *doesn't*, want to limp for forever time like Johnny. If she wants to be able to stand.

I've money saved, she tells me, *enough for a week in a boarding house in town.* But the doctor said she needs four whole weeks. The doctor says she needs another job. She says she could work in a hotel in Boulder, share up the heavy work with others. Days there not as long as here.

Our sleeping room feels woven tight, thick with words and hard to the breath. Money for the boarding house room. Money for the train to town. Money for the doctor. Ma's money is not enough. My 50-cent piece is not enough.

When Ma sleeps hard, I pull on my boots and coat and walk myself outside, behind the bunk house. The moon is round, a bright miner's lantern for the above. Through open windows, I hear miners snore—rocks dragged on rough ground.

I go to the slanted land and spotted rock and dig where Otis Farnley dug. The earth is soft. Not far down is an old bucket filled with wrinkled dollars and cold coins. I take it all.

I pull off my neckerchief, shake it loose, empty the monies into it and tie it into a bundle. I throw pay man's bucket into the creek. It swallows water and sinks.

In a tight spot near the train trestle and tree roots, I dig with a sharp rock, narrow and deep. I hear a noise in the trees and stop. It is only a deer, restless in its sleep.

I relocate part of the dollars and part of the coins into a can I find in the ravine. I sniff it and smell peaches. I sink it in the hole.

I bury more dollars and more coins in more cans. In different places, which I remember inside the holes in my brain.

The next morning, I am like the tailing pile: crumbling, splintery inside. To align myself, I find grasses to put in order, tall to short. Mr. Farnley walks past. Thick to thin. He spits on the ground. Bristly to soft to bristly.

That night, Ma says, "Adder?" when I arise from my bedding, but returns right to asleep. I dig at the broken-arm tree and at the low wall. I leave three coins for Mr. Farnley in one bucket, enough for a coach ride into town. In the other bucket, I leave pine cones, in no alignment at all.

All in the all, I rebury his money in six new spaces. No one follows me. Only the aspen trees watch.

Pay day again, and after cheating five men—four dollars, three, and one, one, one—Mr. Farnley drinks whiskey until dusk time, upon which, he departs the bunk house to bury his money.

From behind a thorn shrub, I watch him dig. I see him squeezed hard by confusion. He's cursing softly. He's cursing loudly. He swallows more whiskey and runs stumbly from the slanted land to the stone wall to the broken-arm tree, kicking rocks and trunks. He throws his empty bottle at a mining barrow.

Frankie, Sal, and Big Clyde, scrubbed clean and rigging a buckboard to go to town, ask him what the shouts and curses are for. *Somebody!* he yells, *Somebody!*—but then shuts himself up. Why would a pay man bury money? How could he have so many dollars and coins? Even a boy like me knows not to talk about money you shouldn't have.

I sit invisible in the dirt, aligning tin cans.

Big Clyde tells him to dry out and throws him a horse blanket. Otis Farnley stomp stomps off, gone to sleep in the cheatgrass.

Early morning, Sunday morning, he's wild in the bunk room, pulling off sheets, flipping mattresses, yelling "Where is it?! Who's got it?" He only finds flasks, nudie magazines, and scowling men, sleeping into daylight the only day they can.

Nedda and Johnny set into town to find Head Man. Big Clyde, Sturdy Joe, Sal, and Skinny Nat (Nat the Rat, some call him because he presses into places no one else can fit) lock Mr. Farnley in the storeroom with boards nailed over the door. We listen to fists banging and cans hitting the wall, then nothing. Later, when Head Man reaches the bunkhouse, Big Clyde pries the boards off the door and Mr. Farnley runs like an elk at Head Man and knocks him over. Yells, "You took it. You!"

Johnny says Mr. Farnley drank bad drink. Skinny Nat says Mr. Devil's crawled under Farnley's flesh. Mr. Head Man says to tie him like a hog and drive him to town. I say nothing.

They rope Otis Farnley's hands and feet and sit him in the horse cart. Nat tells me they'll put him in a jail cell until the devil moves on.

After Ma and me clean the store room, after she goes to sleep and I make as if I am, I take an empty flour sack from the kitchen. Outside, the moon is not as round as it could be, but it is enough. I dig out the cans of money. I take all but one, as a just in case.

Night is still night when I awake up Ma and tell her how Mr. Farnley cheated the men and buried the money and how I watched him and undug it and now it is ours. "We can go to town and you can rest your foot," I whisper. Then I open the flour sack. She makes a surprised sound and I think maybe a mouse crawled in but no it was all those coins and bills.

"But Edward," she says, "this money isn't ours. It belongs to the miners."

I hadn't reflected on that. I only thought of taking from the pay man, not the men he'd taked from before. I tell Ma I didn't recollect the numbers of all whose money it was and some might be Mr. Farnley's real pay and also to remember some of the mining men whose pay got taken did not mine at Blue Bird anymore.

Ma thought a while, then she said we needed to count all the miners plus Nedda. That made fourteen to which we added the two of us for sixteen all together. I aligned the money, most to least paper, most to least coins. We built the monies into even piles with the extra over for Nedda since she helped with the cooking.

The next day, when the men were in the mines and Mr. Farnley was in his jail, I helped Ma tie the money and coins in butcher paper and lay the parcels in each man's bed and in Nedda's too. Then we went to the kitchen to open cans and cut turnips for supper. I was all jumpity inside so Ma said, "Adder, why don't you align the turnips?"

There will be clamor and tumult when Nedda and the men find their parcels. Laughing and whooping and only a little asking. For some men, the parcels are but a part of what's owed them. For other men, a real money bonus. For Ma and me, enough to leave, heal some, start again.

The day before we go, I stand on the ground, aligning rusted nails on the bunkhouse porch. Thick to narrow. Narrow to thick. Sharp to dull. Dull to sharp, sharp, sharpest.

The Miner

1877

JEREMIAH SAYS IT'S the chill of an open grave. Skinny Nat calls it the musty mouth of hell, the breath of the Devil himself.

Me? I think the mine opening smells like my uncle's root cellar, back in Ohio. Two thousand miles away from this heavenly damnation.

Paradoxical, isn't it? The valley at Blue Bird is the most magnificent land I've seen since I crossed the stateline—Dalmatian mountains, white-trunked trees with fluttering leaves, God's own blue sky. Where do I spend my days? Plunged into Lucifer's den.

It's not the arduous toil work I mind. I'm a farm boy. I know how to work hard. What I wasn't ready for was the darkness. Somehow, I thought we'd leave the mine for our mid-day meal and an afternoon cup of java. Certainly, to relieve ourselves. No, sir.

The cold surprised me too. How quick the chill after sunset, even here in October. We wake at six, pull our filthy flannel shirts over our long johns, our canvas cover-alls over them both. Half-awake or less, we load gruel and mush into our mouths, swallow, do it again. We eat a hardboiled egg, two if we're lucky. We wash it down with something thick that tastes nothing like coffee, but it doesn't matter because it's hot.

Then it's outside to watch the morning spread across the valley, to drink in the light like you drank in that coffee, for you will need both to survive the next ten hours. It's cold outside. It's cold in the tunnels. You warm as you work, then you are chilled by your own sweat.

In August, the work was acceptable because they assigned me to just inside the entrance, loading rocks into carts, wheeling them to the tiling pile. My shoulders hurt, but my arms grew strong. Some days I welded, repairing broke wheels and busted picks, praising God that Uncle Caleb taught me to work the fire before he'd died. The welding offered focus to my mind and relief to my back.

Then Clayton, who said little but was a man a fellow could rely upon, shattered his shoulder. A single misjudgment out of a thousand right ones and now he's weak-armed for life. Down I went to take his place, into the shaft, boots laced hard, candle at the ready.

Below, we are changed souls. Shadow and flat form, colorless motion, breaking, pulling, loading. A man can take a single step out of the torch light and wholly disappear. It spooks.

The tunnels are dark, frosty, and sometimes wet by seepage. They always stink. The men relieve themselves in corners, leave behind the high smell of urine and excrement, of alcohol vomited on a Monday morning. The lumber shoring up ceilings and walls can be slippery, splintered, or altogether rotten. Nails protrude.

My fourth week below, I thought of Plato and his cave, with its prisoners, fire, and shadows. What is real and what is imagined and who is to say which is which? We read *The Republic* my tenth year of schooling, before I quit to take Uncle Caleb's place at the farm, beaten down as he was by pneumonia. I didn't understand Plato then. Even the school master, Mr. Trammel, taught us that the work was full of mystery. The point of the tale was to ask questions, to ruminate upon them.

I didn't understand the shadows then. I do now.

I thought of Plato only the fourth week because my first three weeks, I thought of nothing. Those weeks, I simply strove to bear the blisters, the bright streaks of pain, the stiffness, the ink.

Time dragged by. I learned how to work despite the sharp aches. Worse, was the boredom.

Our farm demanded of us, but there was an arc to its labor. Plowing, planting, sprouting, tending, harvesting. Fecundity. Shifting light and changing color. At Blue Bird, I often wake in blackness, always work in blackness, take my evening meal in dusky shadows. I remember my astonishment last month, when we had entered the mine with remarks on the fair morning only to emerge at day's end to a half-foot of snow. What a strange land these mountains are.

Here, it is the community of men that allows one to survive. At first, my comrades seemed a species apart—rougher in language, paltry in character, and far more sturdy. As the days passed, I better met them and I could see most were, or could be, brothers in Christ. Even the Papists! Some of the harder fellows could have used the guidance of Sunday worship, over the hill in Caribou (and Johnny has become a friend in this way), but I am no proselytizer.

True, the cook's son, Edward, sometimes asks me to read to him from the Holy Book, and that I do, because he is young and he asked. Edward is an odd one, always arranging scattered what-not—pine cones, potatoes, broken branches—but he's polite, listens thoughtfully, and works hard. The one who fills and doles out our lunch buckets, he's precise and ready each day break. He'll make a fine fellow, in his own way.

Edward calls me *Ohio Bill*. Upon my arrival, he'd explained that there had been three Williams before me and that to make an order of us, we needed distinct names. "Ohio Bill" suits me. It reminds me that I am a farmer, not a miner. That the blackness is not forever. That I will not be like the others who spend their lives removed from the sun.

In the darkness, one must listen. I learn each man's voice, his swing and his step, so I don't startle or become startled or misjudge. Shattered shoulder. Cut calf. Lost finger. We must watch out for each other.

Men have their scents which grow stronger as the week passes. Three sets of clothes if you are lucky: two for work, one for Sundays. We bathe on Saturday nights and we also drink on Saturday nights, those of us who drink, which I do not. Some, like Marco and Dickie Smyth, grab the buckboard and head to Cardinal for more liquor and ladies.

Some of us who refrain from drink make this time our time to prepare for the holy day. We bathe, as I said. We shake out our sheets and blankets, sweep as we can.

On a rare Saturday night, I read a letter that has, with God's hand, made its way from home. More often, I'll contemplate a gospel verse as the ruckus of the men's card game rises through the floor boards. I sit on my pallet in the bunk room and, through the weak light of an oil lamp, gaze at pictures pasted onto the wall: sweethearts, family, and, for many, the faces of girls cut out of the weeklies.

Come Sunday, some men sleep, most drink, and a few fish, when the weather approves of it. A handful take a horse and cart into town to worship. Our Sunday prayers are a mean affair, sometimes a man of the cloth guiding us in a bare room in a Caribou boarding house, sometimes just we brothers, sharing word and spirit.

After prayers, I give most of my pay to Miss Todd, the boarding house proprietress, who brings it to Nederland for banking. Sometimes, if my body is not too broken, I forgo the horse and walk back from town, giving me time for reflection on the Lord's word or to ponder my own state of affairs.

Surely, I didn't intend this life when I fled my birth place. Once my father and uncles took over Uncle

Caleb's farm, they mistreated and mistrusted each other to such lengths that they pulled the entire concern under. With the War between the States only nine years behind us, you'd have thought they'd seen enough brutality. They needn't have cooked up more amongst family.

I was no longer a boy at seventeen but not enough of a man to hold my own stead against them. As such, a year later, I escaped west with bold imaginings but little forethought. "Quitter," my uncles had called me, as I hoisted myself onto a farmer's wagon bound for Findlay.

Months later, in the newly-minted state of Colorado, near Fort Lupton, Fort Morgan, and many a hamlet in-between, I put in my time with beef cattle, railcar loading, haying. One morning, having slept beneath a cottonwood I'd come upon the day before, just as the last of the dusk surrendered to darkness, I awoke near a fine red barn. Above me, a small herd of Brown-Swiss and Holsteins stared with great interest. Beyond them, I heard the giggles of three girls, whom I would soon know as Alice, Hattie, and the curly-headed Minnie, pointing to my union suit. My face, I am sure, grew as red as my under-garments, and hastily, I pulled my blanket around me.

Their mother, Mrs. Garber, arrived, offering me a wet rag and a hot breakfast. In exchange, I gave the family my day, mucking stalls and fixing a broken fence railing. This arrangement suited us all, including Mr. Garber, who had a shared interest in a general store in Platteville, two miles away.

That evening I slept in the barn, sweet hay all around me, and again the next day offered my services. I stayed for two weeks, performing all matter of chores, including helping birth the Holstein's first calf, whom Alice named "Willy" in my honor. I left on a Sunday with freshly-laundered clothes, an extra blanket, and a round of soft cheese, straight from Maudine, the largest of their Brown-Swiss.

In the depth of the silver mine, I think of that small farm often. Its whitewashed fences and soft-eyed cows, but especially those family suppers. Especially Alice's glances. I envision Colorado's abounding sunlight spilling down on them all.

We are given our weekly wages on Saturdays, the paymaster doling out bills. The first time, old Farnley tried to cheat me, claiming hogwash about "an apprentice salary," three bills less than agreed. I am not a large fellow, I lack the muscle and heft of others, but swindlers ignite my ire. Enflame my stubborn streak.

"I've known my fill of charlatans," I told Farnley, "and I'm peering at one presently. You will give me my pay, full and as promised." He concocted again his reasons for short-changing me. I stopped him cold. "Now and all," I said, "or I will question every man here how far your deception reaches."

He gave me what was owed.

I questioned the men still. Some turned away, others swore they had no gripe with Farnley, but I could tell many had been fleeced, black-mailed somehow into silence. I let the matter go but kept both eyes on the paymaster.

The days grew shorter. On a brisk Sunday morning, two men left, Dickie and Nunzio, unwilling to endure another winter at Blue Bird. The mine owner, afraid the lot of us would take flight, rode to the bunkhouse the next evening and promised us a bonus.

Part of me thought Nunzio and Dickie wise—why did I continue on? Beyond steady work and steady food, which had enticed me to the mountain, no reason beyond my own mulish mind compelled me to stay, a self-promise to remain until I had saved enough to apply for land of my own.

At the farm, Mrs. Garber had explained how, when I reached the age of twenty-one, I could submit myself for the Homesteading Act. It was through this act that they had acquired their farm and, same on, that I could benefit. It wasn't enough, Mr. Garber told me, to save solely the requirement that the government papers demanded, but to salt away a reserve for rough patches and hard times that would surely present themselves before I proved up. By my count, one more year here and I will have sufficient funds to commence my larger undertaking.

My comrades' leavings turn me though. Surely, I can find other opportunities in the valley.

Midwinter, and the cook is the next to vanish. His wife, Alma, works in his stead. The food shows considerable improvement, richer in taste and more abundant. This is welcome by all.

The promised bonus? It vanishes as well. I suspect Otis Farnley has his malevolent hand in this but when the boys and I press him, he blames the mine owner. There's grumbling and one more man packs his duffle and heads out.

As the days warm, a handful of men take their supper to the bunkhouse porch, hungry for scraps of light. Swallowing their stew and chewing their chicken bones, some brag about women, some about bears, a few argue the politics of the day. I listen as Nat, Marco, and Big Clyde debate the nature of mining. Nat praises Blue Bird as God's gift to us, a wonder of rock and ore to be mined and milled for the advancement of man.

"Silver bands, gold watches—what advancement is that?" Big Clyde wants to know. He judges there's something wrong with all this taking and taking, boring into the earth. Clyde was a farmer too, growing wheat in Kansas. Marco and Clyde commence to argue whether farming is not its own violation, forcing the soil to produce for our own benefit.

Clyde counters that good farmers add manure and fish meal to the soil and let a field sit fallow to regain its strength. A mine cannot do that. Marco says the earth does not need its silver, gold, and coal. Would you walk past a coin fallen on the ground? Their talk reminds me of Plato's cave. It's all how we see things and who is to say what is right?

What is true is that tomorrow morning we will lace our boots and descend into the "deep down under," as our Edward has so baptized those dark chambers.

Weeks later, late spring, we emerge from the mine before noon. A tunnel wall has collapsed and while we all are alive, Marco's arm hangs unnaturally, and a new man, Floyd, a boy, really, bleeds from his forehead. As Marco is fed whiskey and bundled off to town, I wash at the rain barrel. There I see Edward's wiggly line of ore, small chunks that Johnny brought him yesterday. Edward explains, though I already know, that the blue streaks are azurite.

Streaks. My own stubborn streak. I've always imagined it red, like the run of blood on Floyd's face. Maybe it is blue. Edward has arranged the rocks so that the streaks roughly touch from edge to edge. They look like a creek. A trail. Am I too stubborn to leave? Am I afraid to be again called a quitter?

Who is doing the calling?

"Father," I ask, taking one of the rocks into my hand, "what am I to do?"

The mine is shut for a week as engineers reinforce the ceiling. It fails. As a new route is dug, we are sent through an older route, longer and more taxing.

Trouble comes in threes, Uncle Caleb used to say, and that week Alma drops a soup pot on her foot. She walks with a cane now, until the bones heal. She needs to rest, but she needs the pay.

Otis Farnley relishes the damage, taunting and badgering. I don't know if I entirely believe in the devil, but if Lucifer *is* real, he must be a friend of the paymaster. Johnny, Sturdy Joe, and I try to keep an eye on Farnley, but some nights I'm too dog-tired to do anything but eat and climb the creaking stairs to the bunk room. *This damned, damned place,* I think.

The most bewildering occurrence has overtaken us. On Saturday, Otis Farnley turned maniacal, digging in the dirt as would an over-wrought dog. Rumors abounded— bad drink, hydro-phobia, Satan's own possession? Big Clyde sent him off to sleep in the trees.

Then yesterday morning, Sunday morning, Farnley roared up the stairs to the bunk room, jerking back blankets, tearing off bed sheets, yelling, "Who took it?!" Four men held him while the mine owner was summoned. He hauled Farnley to a jail cell in Caribou. Dinner was quiet. The men talked in low voices, if at all. We helped Alma scrape dishes and throw out the refuse.

This morning, we awoke as standard, laced our boots and lined up for the mine. Edward handed me my lunch bucket. He looked waxen, his knuckles rubbed raw. *This damned place,* I again whispered.

I was among the last to leave the mine in the afternoon and as I crossed the narrow field, I heard shouting from the bunk house. I reasoned that Farnley had returned, but as I grew nearer, I also heard laughter. In the bunk room, Johnny reached for a brown paper parcel on my bed and held it out to me. I pulled off the twine and coins spilled out, leaving a bundle of paper bills in my hand.

Johnny motioned his hand wide. "One for each soul. Even Alma and Nedda. Even Edward."

"Where did it come from?" I asked. I laid the bills on the blanket.

"Don't know," Johnny said.

"God or the devil," Nat called out. "Don't matter which."

"One hundred and forty-four dollars to a man!" Salvador told me, picking up my fallen coins and handing them to me. "Nearly six weeks' pay."

"If we was ever paid right," Nat said and silence cut through the room.

No one is sleeping much tonight and I imagine crew numbers will be scanter tomorrow. I will be one man making them so. Sitting here on the creek bank, listening to its roar and tumble, I tilt my head toward the thousand stars of heaven. I'd asked the Lord for guidance, hadn't I? How could this be anything else?

When I lace my boots before daybreak, I won't be walking into the mouth of hell. I'll be wearing my Sunday best on a Tuesday, my kit sack and bedroll strapped to my back, walking to Caribou's best boarding house. I envision a long night's rest there, and maybe a second. A hot bath for certain. A visit to the bank. After that, a stagecoach to Boulder followed by a visit to a certain farm, two miles west of Platteville.

"God or the devil," I repeat to myself as the creek tumbles on. I recall Otis Farnley trying to cheat me out of my wages. I remember the promised bonus that never arrived. Two days ago, Otis digging like a dog. I bring to mind Edward's hands as he held my lunch bucket. Knuckles raw. Flesh scraped.

God. The Devil. Or maybe a boy.

The Artist

1912

I HAVE RIDDEN trains before, you know. Daddy used to be a Pullman Porter on the Boston to Baltimore run. Sometimes, he took me along. Mama did not like this, declaring that my father smuggled me on as if I were a "valise filled with whiskey."

"She should see the world," Daddy retorted, and, on this matter, he always won.

"It'll bring trouble," Mama warned him, but it was a different trouble that brought us here.

My longest train ride was our trip west. Three trains to be precise. (Mama says precision brings progress so I will be precise.) Eighteen months ago, we rode past grimy cities, brick-building towns, and canvas-tent hobo camps. Past hilly cow fields, flat crop fields, piled-high junk yards, and crows gripping telephone wires so tight Mama said they were making calls of their own.

Sitting tall by window, I watched our county pass by. Mama, beside me, closed her eyes and hummed softly to the baby inside her. In the aisle seat, Daddy read *Up From Slavery*, frequently quoting passages aloud. Aside from Mama and me, Daddy loves Booker T. Washington most.

On occasion, Mama and Daddy pointed to a faded map, showing me when, for an example, we passed from Ohio to Indiana or from Iowa to Nebraska. But crossing lines on paper does not guarantee change outside the train window. Other times, a big change, the way the earth flattened or sky widened, wasn't on the map at all.

When the train stopped in Cleveland, I asked if we could disembark there. *Disembark,* that's the name for leaving the train, although when I hear it, I think of a tree shedding its skin. In Pittsburgh, I had pleaded to take a train back to Philadelphia, to a different neighborhood if necessary, but not too far from the people I knew. Miss Helene, one floor above, who knitted hats and told stories about New Orleans. The Johnson family, one floor below, where I played dolls with Rebecca and practiced spelling with Howard. But Mama said Daddy's new job was in Denver and so Denver it was and after Chicago I stopped asking.

We couldn't go back to Philadelphia on account of Daddy, who, on a train north of Baltimore, had not answered a white man the way that white man wanted. When the white man called out *Boy* and my father didn't answer, the man called again and this time louder.

Can I help you, Sir? my father's boss had said, stepping into the car.

I didn't answer because I thought you were speaking to your son, my father explained to the white man. *I thought when you said* Boy, *you meant your boy.*

That made sense to me, a boy is a boy and my father is a man. Anyone who can count years or has eyes sees that. But the white man was important, important and angry, and he didn't believe my father when my father said he was not a boy.

That is how my father lost his job on the railroad.

I thought it was all railroads where Daddy couldn't work until Daddy's friend, Mr. Eddie, got him a job fixing and cleaning cars for the Burlington Railroad in Denver. Like Daddy, Mr. Eddie was quiet and thin and liked to read Booker T. Washington.

On the morning we arrived, three days before Christmas, ten years into the new century, the sky was bluer than I ever remember seeing, the air bright cold. Denver wasn't at all like Philadelphia—cleaner but also muddier, old-fashioned and newer at the same time. In the distance, mountains.

We stepped off the train and were suddenly poor: me, Daddy, Mama and the baby inside her. We slept on an old mattress in Mr. Eddie's front room above a shoe repair shop.

When, on New Year's Day, I told Mama and Daddy I missed home terribly, Daddy advised me to stand tall, quoting from Mr. Washington: *Nothing ever comes to one except as a result of hard work*. There are all kinds of hard work, he told me, including that of living in a new land.

Mama pulled me close. "You'll find your life here, by and by," she promised.

In January, I started the fourth grade with other Negro and Mexico children and also two white ones who were even poorer than us. On Saturday mornings, I joined the line of children selling scavenged cans to the scrap man. On Saturday afternoons, my father, if he hadn't secured extra work that day, walked me to the library. On Sundays, we all went to church.

In our house, once chores were done, reading was admired, even expected. On days when Mama took in sewing, Daddy would read aloud to her while she made her careful stitches. I read whatever I could borrow or find that week—*The Secret Garden, The Wizard of Oz, Uncle Tom's Cabin*—I would sometimes see Daddy standing over me. He'd nod and repeat what Mr. Washington's words, "If you can't read, it's hard to realize dreams."

I read so much my eyes got soft and I couldn't see the far-away world as sharply as before. I moved to the front row of my classroom. I squinted as blurred neighbors walked toward me. I began memorizing their stride and bearing. Mama said "eyeglasses someday," when we had money again. That was all right. I had my books.

Reading carried me away from my world, but drawing drew me into it. In March, old Mr. Abrams, who lived above the dry goods store across the street, taught me about sketching. On warm afternoons, we sat on wood chairs on the sidewalk, or, on cooler day, in a corner of the store, now owned by his son. Mr. Abrams showed me how to hold my pencil, emphasizing the importance of shape and shadow. He watched as I drew cross-contour lines, hatching and crosshatching to create depth. I learned when to draft lightly and when to press hard.

With Mr. Abrams' *American Drawing-Book* in one hand, I walked our block, squinting when I needed to, sketching the people of Welton Street. Big-muscled Mr. Hutnik, the ice man. Mr. Clifford, his hair tied back, who cooked at the Baxter Hotel. Mustached Mr. Lawrence, on his stoop, smoking a cigar. Friendly Mr. Holmes, who collected death insurance payments. Barbara and Betsy, the cinnamon twins, skipping rope. That's what we called them because that's what they called themselves, proud of their light skin.

Mama didn't disapprove of my drawings but she didn't ask to see them and she didn't bring me pencils and rubbing erasers like Daddy did. "I keep my eye out for them on the walk to the station," he'd tell me. "I know it's going to be a good day when I find one." While Mama would have preferred I spend my sketching time stitching a quilt or mending my father's work clothes, she let me be.

The weather got warmer, Mama got fatter, and we moved to a nearby set of rooms one block away. The flat was above a laundry, the hiss hiss of the pressing machine rising through the floorboards. The baby was born in early May. My father named him Taliaferro after the "T" in Booker T. We called him Ferro. I drew a picture of him in his cradle and gave it to Mama.

Now it's a year later (one year and nine weeks, to be precise) and I am to enter the sixth grade come August and Ferro is a chubby baby, gone from crawling on the rag rugs that cover our rough floors to walk-waddling across them. The air in our small apartment is hot and the faucet water comes out rusty sometimes, but our family is happy because Daddy, along with cleaning and repairing train cars, is working as a porter again.

He's not wholly a porter because his new train does not have sleeping cars and his new job is only for a few months. Still, he and Mama are grateful for the work and I like the name of the special train: The Switzerland Trail. It is called that even though it is not in Switzerland, but right here in Colorado. Daddy says I might think I am in Switzerland once I ride it. Four weeks later, he brings me a ticket. I am going to be a passenger on the Switzerland Trail.

When I rode the train between Boston and Baltimore, while Daddy Pullman-Portered, I walked the cars until I found a Negro woman or Negro family to sit next to. If the train filled while I was sitting down, I'd stand until someone disembarked.

Once, my mother and I rode the train together, for real, with tickets, from Philadelphia to Charleston to visit Grandma Patterson. In Baltimore, heading south, the train men added a Negro car and Mama and I had to move there where the seats were harder, the floors dirtier, and windows filmier from the coal and dust flying out the engine. I looked straight ahead as we walked forward, remembering what Mr. Washington said: *Character is power.*

On the train ride home from Charleston, the segregation loosened in Baltimore and Negros and whites could sit in the same cars again, but my mother said to stay in the Negro car. It was safer.

All the passengers on the Switzerland Trail train are white. Most of them are dressed in white. I am wearing my good blue dress. I have a real seat, by a right-side window. For this reason, I don't mind too much the women's surprised stares, the men's frowns, or the children's giggles when they see me. I hold up my chin and nod, as my father and Mr. Washington have taught me to do. *Success is to be measured by the obstacles we overcome.*

I don't see trunks or boxes or valises on the train. "No fancy hotels where we're going," my father says.

"To Zurich?" I ask. He knows I am making a joke.

The train heads into the space between the mountains. Misty, purple mountains majesty, same as we sing in class. Outside, the sky is blue, same as that first day.

I think of our neighbor, Mr. Clifford, whose portrait I sketched when I was still ten. When he was little, he followed a rabbit into the brush. As he tried to touch the rabbit, a bear cub peered out from behind a boulder. His brothers, who'd been following, scooped him up and took him back to his family. "I didn't know to be scared, he told me. "I wanted to see that bear."

I wonder if I will see a bear today, here from this safe train. Mr. Clifford's people, the Arapaho, have lived here for hundreds of years. Some of them must have walked the trail this train is now traveling. They saw many bears, I am sure.

The town below grows smaller and disappears. I've never been so close to mountains before. They are not rounded triangles the way I drew them in fourth grade. Also, although my sight is soft—near-sighted is the medical word for it—I can tell, when we stop or go slow around a bend, that the mountains are made of pine trees, trees with white trunks, and a creek that goes on and on. Birds live here. We pass red station houses with names like story titles: Two Brothers. Black Swan. Tambourine. A white-spotted deer approaches the train while we stop in a town called Sunset. "He's been tamed," my father whispers, pretending to adjust a latch in the compartment above my head.

Outside, the air is cool, a different world of air than in our apartment. "I want to touch everything," I tell my father.

"Soon," he says, smiling. He hasn't smiled like that in a long time.

A few minutes before noon, the track cuts through more trees and over North Boulder Creek where the train slows. "Blue Bird Mine, next stop!" my father calls, then walks down the aisle, passing out picnic baskets. Outside, is an open valley.

The train stops. In their white dresses and white linen suits, with their hats, hiking sticks and baskets, the white passengers stand and fill the aisle. I stay seated. One of the women looks at me, whispers to her husband, but not so quietly that I can't hear. "Look, Jackson, a pickaninny." To the two children who follow, she says, "Don't stare. It isn't polite."

I know they are wrong, I know my worth, but tears rush to my eyes still. I want to turn away, to stare out the window, but I remain steady. I watch them leave, a line of puffy clouds chatting about the fine day ahead.

As the last one walks past me, I see my father in the doorway, lifting his chin. That's his signal to stay above such matters as thoughtless white women. They will not ruin my ride on the Switzerland Trail, my day in the mountains.

"Ruth," Daddy says, once the passengers have left, "Marshall and I will ride to Cardinal and Eldora before we turn the engine back to Blue Bird. What I want you to do..." he reaches onto a compartment and brings down a basket, "is to take this lunch and walk back along the track until you see a stone wall near a large flat rock. You stay there, eat your meal, look at the hills, and breathe this good air. The train will pass you in a few minutes, on its way to Cardinal and then you'll see us again on our return. We'll be by in two hours. Don't wander far."

"I understand," I say, excited to receive a picnic basket like the others. He also hands me two corked bottles of cherry cola, except they are the wrong color. "It's only water," he tells me, "but you'll want it." I take them as he walks me to the platform.

My father kisses me on the forehead, then points me toward the rock and fence. For me, though, everything is patches of color. I know the rock and fence will take their form as I near them. As our front gate does. As does the black board in school. I look back one more time. "If it rains," my father calls after me, "return to the boarding house porch."

I think of my mother, how she would not approve of any of this, a girl sitting in a strange place, *sitting on a rock!*, by herself. But I trust Daddy.

After a few minutes, the train passes me and I wave in case Daddy is waving. Then I make my way down the pink-red path between stands of grasses. Colors are splashed onto the green and I want to stop and look, because I've never seen so many pinks, yellows, and purples sprinkled about. I keep walking until a grey shape tightens into a flat rock, a stone wall materializing behind it.

Kneeling next to the rock, I finger a blue-purple blur whose soft edges tighten into narrow bells. Around me, splatters of colors take shape: ovals, funnels, stars, and cones. Some flowers are colors within colors. Purple petals circle a yellow disk. Yellow petals surround black.

I feel as if I am in the picture book Mama brought home from the house where she cleaned last winter.

Three pages torn out—that's why the family threw it away—but fairies, rabbits, and fields of flowers filled the pages that remained.

As I look at the flowers, wishing I had brought my drawing pad, wishing I owned a magnifying glass like the one we shared in school, my stomach growls. I have forgotten to eat. The picnic basket is packed not with a Sunday dinner as the other passengers received, but with food Mama has prepared. I know this as soon as I see the cloth square below the wicker lid. "Your mama's food is better than anything you'll find onboard," Daddy regularly told me in response to my request to eat in dining cars, in which, I now understand, we are not allowed.

Here, in this meadow, though, surrounded by this blur, not blur, of wildflowers, none of that matters. The high air makes my meal—winter sausage, corn muffins, a small jar of cherry jam and a wrinkled apple—taste especially delicious. I drink half the water from one bottle, save the rest.

When I reach for the second muffin, I hear a crinkly noise beneath the napkin lining the basket. Daddy loves surprises, hiding spearmint candies, horehound drops, and nearly new pencils for me around our house. I remove the cloth to find a small, hand-stitched workbook.

The cover reads Mountainside Flowers of the Sub Alpine. Below that, handwritten, is Mary "Florence" Anderson, Grinnell College, Iowa, 1912. On a half-sheet of paper, tucked inside, I see my father's strong, slanted handwriting: *Yours now, Ruth. Love, Daddy.*

The first two pages of the workbook show four thin black frames, each containing one flower, inked and painted by hand, Mary Florence's hand, I imagine, and labeled with carefully printed words I understand and words I do not. *Rudbeckia hirta*. Black-eyed Susan. *Allium geyeri*. Geyer [Wild] Onion. *Penstemon virens*. Low Penstemon. *Bistorta Bistortoides*. Snakeweed or Knotweed.

The next page has three drawings inside its frames: Harebell, Bedstraw, and Chiming Bell, and one, unlabeled, only inked in. The following pages have frames only. These pages, I understand, are for me.

The basket also holds two pencils, a new eraser, and my tiny sharpening knife. I think of all the paper my father has found for me since we arrived in Denver—handbills, posted announcements fallen off walls, the backs of train schedules. For Christmas, he'd given me a drawing pad.

I think of the neighbors I've drawn. Mrs. Cooper, carrying two satchels of groceries. Terrance Grishold, playing marbles with his brother Tommy. Mr. Abrams, who sometimes calls me *Bisl Blum*. That's his language for "Little Flower."

If I lived here, flowers would be my neighbors.

Flowers should be easier to draw than people because flowers don't move, but when I look closely, there's much detail. The stem is not smooth but covered with fine hairs. When I look at the petals, at first, I just see colored shapes. Keep staring and veiny lines appear.

Miniature stalks reach out in the middle of the petals. Mrs. Vincent, my Sunday school teacher, said God has names for all plants and creatures. I will ask her the name of this insect-like antenna.

The sun is overhead now and I finish drinking from the first cherry cola bottle. Dabbing the sweat on my forehead, I begin drawing a heart-shaped, pink-petaled flower with a yellow center, then a droopy dark-purple flower, then a white flower that looks like the trumpet Joshua's army blew at Jericho, slender at first then flaring into a five-pointed star. I don't have water-color paints with me, I don't own any paints at all, so I do what Mary Florence did for the flowers she had not yet colored. I draw slender arrows to its different parts and, in tiny letters, write reminders: BRIGHT YELLOW WITH PALE GREEN STEM. PURPLE-BLACK. WHITE TURNING TO PINK.

For Christmas this year, I will ask my father for watercolors.

Stretching my neck, I see movement far down the road. Could it be a bear? As I stare, I hear a clop-clopping sound and know it must be horses. Two people nearing on horseback. I stand, gripping my pencil. I think of Cousin Claude, who was doing nothing but drinking a cold soda on a hot day when three white men gave him a beating. His left arm still droops at his side.

The man on the horse raises his hat. "Good day, Miss," he calls in an extra-fancy way.

"You're an artist," the second rider, a woman, says. "A field sketcher." It is hard to see her face in the shadow of her riding hat.

"Yes, ma'am," I say. I hope they don't ask to see my drawings because they might think that I stole the booklet from Mary Florence.

"What a keen idea," she continues. "There's no better way to learn the flora."

My heart tightens then, because I think she said *Florence*, not *flora*.

"Flora?" I repeat.

"*Flora* is the Latin word for plants," she tells me, the same way a teacher would.

"Thank you," I say. "I'm always pleased to learn something new." Mama has instructed me to say this to my elders, and to all white people, even when I am not pleased and even when I already know what they think is new to me.

The man says, "What an outstanding year it is for flowers."

"Yes, sir."

His horse stamps its front legs. The man pats him on his neck, says *There, there, boy*. He asks, "Did you arrive on the Switzerland Trail?"

"I did, sir."

I nearly tell them my Daddy works on the train, but my parents have instructed me to keep my answers short when talking to white people. Then, without thinking, I ask, "May I pet your horses?" The couple says yes, so I pet the brown horse with the white marks and the tan horse whose coat is the same color as a stray dog on our block. "They smell better than the horses in

41

Denver," I tell them, remembering those animals' sad eyes, surrounded by flies.

The couple says their horses are named Buck and Daisy. They tell me they are visiting friends at the Frenchman's Ranch in the valley below. I would have been glad to hear the woman ask *Would you like to ride Daisy?* but she does not. She does say, "We hope to see you again," which was kind.

As I watch them go, I imagine riding the Switzerland Trail train again and the couple meeting me at the platform with an extra horse and the three of us riding to the ranch house where we drink ice tea on the porch.

For now, though, warm water from a cherry cola bottle is just fine. I uncork the second bottle and take small sips. I sketch more flowers from different angles, keeping an eye out for bears since I did see horses and I do want to tell Mr. Clifford that I saw a bear.

I don't see a bear but I do see the blur of a cottontail shortly before the train rumbles through, whistle blowing. I can tell Mr. Clifford that.

In the distance, I see Daddy walking my way. He grins when he reaches me. "I'd give my girl a hug, but I'm dusty from loading supplies." I hand him the rest of the water, which he swallows gladly.

Daddy lowers himself onto the almost flat rock. "We need to walk back soon," he tells me, "but I can sit for a piece. A man has always got to find a moment to sit." He turns his head right and left, as if approving the view. Then he taps the flower book. "Marshall found it last spring, tucked between train seats. No one claimed it." He peers at the cover. "Did you draw anything? Or don't you like to draw anymore?"

I know he is teasing and show him my sketches: circles of petals, bells and funnels, odd spurs and lip-like openings. "I wish I knew all their names."

"Flowers have *two* names," my father tells me, "one in Latin"—he points to the words *Rudbeckia hirta* in Mary Florence's part of the book—"and the common name, Black-eyed Susan." I am surprised my father knows this. "You didn't think your Daddy was so smart, did you?" he asks, smiling. "I was a biology scholar before I left school to start working. Grandpa, of course, was a gardener in Virginia. You knew that, right?"

"Yes, sir."

"A flower has only one Latin name, although the name has two parts, its genus and species. However, that same flower might have a dozen local names." Right then, I think my Daddy would have been a very good teacher. "I memorized the Latin names but common names tell us about the people and not just the flower. This," he points to a flower beside us, "is a blanket flower. And this is Indian paintbrush, but you best believe that a white man concocted that name and that he never asked an Indian what his people called it." He points to a purple one with the yellow center. "What would you name this one?"

"Lavender sunshine," I say.

"And this?" He leans in and I smell the deep earth of coal. He points to a low, white flower comprised of a hundred tiny flowers.

"Lace flower. And this," I say, pointing to the long-tubed white flower, "is Joshua's trumpet."

"I've seen pink varieties too. Some folks call it Fairy Trumpet."

"Fairy Trumpet? I like that even better." I rest my cheek against his shoulder. "Daddy, can we live here? Maybe you could work at the mine or help take care of horses."

"And where would you, Mama, and Ferro live?"

"You could build a house for us. Like Abraham Lincoln's log cabin. I would help. Mr. Clifford and Mr. Abrams—they could help too."

I know we will never move here. Still, the day has been so perfect—the train ride, the drawing book, Daisy and Buck, and the hundreds and hundreds of flowers. I want to stay forever.

"It's a fairy land in summer," Daddy said, "but come winter this valley is buried in snow."

"I'd like to see that too," I say, then add, defiantly, "When I grow up, I'm going to move here and build my *own* cabin. I'll paint flowers and snowflakes and horses and sell the paintings to everyone who rides the Switzerland Trail."

Daddy nods. "It's good to have a plan," he says, but instead of laughter, his voice is distant. On the train to Denver, I heard him tell Mama there is no future for Negroes in America. I wonder if he thinks we all should return to Africa, our true home.

"But, Daddy, this feels like home to me," I tell him, as if we'd been arguing about it.

My father looks puzzled, then says solemnly, "Thank you. I'm always pleased to learn something new." This time he smiles. We both laugh and I reach for the basket and my new sketch book. Daddy takes the empty bottles and we begin walking to the platform. When I grow up, I decide, I will go to college and study plants like Daddy never could.

After a few steps, I turn around, checking to see if I left anything behind. I haven't, but for a moment, I see myself on that nearly flat rock, much older and surrounded by school children. I am teaching to them to draw, to draw and to see. Their neighbors, their streets, these flowers. Beyond.

The Trail Rider

1946

THE FIRST WAS scent. The smell of my mother's milk. The fragrance of her neck and loins. Beyond her, dried grasses and aged wood. Dust in the air and dung on the floor.

Soon after, the smells of the others. Their breath and their bodies—what clung and what they generated from within. Next, the visitors, by the scent of their hair, sweat, tobacco—and their drink. I learned what exhaustion smells like. Also, stealth. Also love.

Sound was second. Bodies scratching against walls. Bodies scratching themselves. The scampering of rats, mice, and voles. Feed poured. Feed eaten. Water slurped. Doors creaking. The groan, as darkness moved in, of the walls and roof settling. Although we possessed more than sound by which to understand each other, I took comfort in my mother's small noises, her swallows and bray, her shuffling hooves, her own night time settling next to me.

I was led into a world without stalls. Vastness overwhelmed me and I anchored against my mother's flank. The next day, we were led out again. A light wind inundated us with scent and sounds—some new, some familiar, some skewed, and all too much at once.

The third day, I smelled dew.

By the fourth, I could better focus, staying out longer, walking, trotting, slower to run than the others as I took in the ridged hard earth, the nearby feeding troughs, the far aspen stand, and the still farther mountains. I learned to see color: flax and bone and gold and cream. Khaki. Umber. Chestnut. Black. My mother's white star between her eyes.

On the fifth day, rain. The sound of it. The smell and wet of it.

On the sixth day, my mother and I were led out earlier and I felt the warmth before I left the barn door. I stared at the ground as we walked. At the edge of the field, I looked up at an intensity I'd not yet experienced. Riveted, I signaled my mother. "What is that?"

"Mother Blue."

"Mother Blue?"

"Mother Blue covers us," she told me.

"Mother Blue is our blanket." This from a yearling.

"Mother Blue is the creator." A mare.

"Mother Blue is our protector." From Qimat, a gelding.

Mother Blue sleeps at night. She visits in the day. She brings the sun. She moves aside to allow the rain. The soundless voices fill my head. The herd teaching me.

This was years ago.

Horses do not communicate as humans do with their jerky stream of noises. Yes, we have our sounds, but we possess measures beyond even what you call telepathy. We sense, of course, fear, excitement, and longing amongst us—what animal does not?—but we also absorb that which other horses smell, hear and see. Sometimes these experiences, these *sensories*, are purposefully directed. More often, free-floating. Sensories arrive from herds near and far, mostly from the living, but some of us commune with horses beyond our physical realm.

As a foal, I was taught to draw in and filter out. Initially, I did not believe I would ever make sense of the layers of time, place, and memory. (Was that whiff of hay from the bale nearby or merely the yearning of a mare who'd stood here two days ago, two years ago, or in another field altogether?) Eventually, I learned what was meant for me and what was merely drifting about. I could differentiate among fresh and timeworn, and the twining of the two. Later, the universality of it all.

I will never outgrow my wonder for Mother Blue. When I was a foal, I looked upward so often that my mother named me Sama, our ancestors' word for sky.

Mother taught me what to taste and what to veer from, where water was clear and where it was tainted. How to stay warm on brisk days and cool when the sun seared the blue. Which ranch hands were decent and kind. How to withstand those who were not. When to be courageous. When to feign docility.

You may know the story of this meadow. A man called Boss bringing us here from lower valleys and shores and, before that, from the sand land beyond the sea. Breeding us in this mountain land. Our memories know-feel-hold the far away, long ago. It is there and it is here, with us.

Mother taught me our purpose: *We are here to make more horses. We are here for the amusement of people. We are here to lead them to beauty.* If you find your place among these three functions, she told me, you may be able to stay. We are not free, she explained, but we are fortunate. We are fed well with green and bright hay. Our alfalfa is free from mold. The new trainer is smarter and more caring than the last. The whip is mostly gone.

She told me, "Draw your strength from this land, its air, and Mother Blue." She sent me images of our ancestors in Arabian desert oases and on green rolling hills with white wooden fences. She sent images of boney mares in muddy lots. Baked-earth pens with limping geldings. I understood my good fortune.

She offered sensories of my brother and sister, both of whom were taken from her because of their beauty, strength, and build. I possess none of these, so I was not taken away. Sometimes it is a gift not to be the most elegant. My brother and sister were far but safe, one living with cattle near water and the other in a lush pasture. My mother missed them.

My mother and I live in these high lands and also the low fields. The ranch hands move us in tin trailers when the days shorten, return us when the days grow long. The mares, colts, and fillies travel up and down. The stallions remain. Boss says it builds character for the stallions to endure the cold. Boss himself doesn't stay.

Winter light is brief in the valley. The stallions grow a dense winter coat. They eat hay hour after hour. They stand close to each other, sharing heat. They wear blankets and bed in the straw or wood shavings. Some nights, none of it is enough and they shake with cold.

Below, on the edges of town, we sense them. We glimpse our green pastures turned white. We send visions of our hot ancestral home, in hopes of cheering them. Sometimes we feel our visions embraced. Other times, they are pushed away in anger.

When we return, some stallions lope across the field to greet us. Others remain distant, out of anger, pride, or disdain. I believe it is Boss' intent to drive us, male and female, apart. He does the same in his own house, treating the females like horses, bodies brought in to amuse and serve him.

Baham is Boss' horse. Large frame. Sturdy build. White coat. He has little grace. Few expansive thoughts. What Boss prefers.

As a yearling, I asked my mother about my father. Was he here in the field? No, he'd been taken east. Did she have an image, a memory of him? She told me of a dark bay stallion, black tail and elegant black stockings, purposeful in his duty. My dark bay father, my bright bay mother, and me, a chestnut with a blond mane and one blond fetlock. Boss gave me barely a glance, but Manuel, a ranch hand, took a liking to me, recognized my value.

When I was a young mare, my mother instructed me to find my near one in the herd. "While you will always be part of the equine universal," she told me, "with your near one, you can experience together what is in this place, in these days granted to us by Mother Blue." She nuzzled my neck. "Listen to the wind as it sets the hay field in motion. Watch the stars appear."

When I told my mother that I required no one but her, she insisted I learn to share my joys and worries. After she was gone, she told me, I would need another to heal the emptiness. I did know she could be taken, by Boss or Mother Blue, at any time, but I pushed that knowledge away.

The gelding Qimat is my mother's near one, the one with whom she watches clouds cross the sky, thunderstorms feed the grasses. Together they have watched brooding mares turn heavy, their foals grow, and in time, give birth to their own young.

As I matured from yearling to filly, I found my near one: Nashirah, my "bringer of good news." With her dark coat and black mane, Nashirah is far more beautiful than I, her white blaze outshining the ivory snip between my nostrils. Yet, Nashirah cares little about appearances. Two weeks younger than me, we learned to run together, to lope, gallop, and jump. She is quicker, but I have more endurance. She can jump higher, but I have more patience. Where I am watchful, she is carefree.

I sometimes envy her, but I know I cannot be any horse other than myself. Still, she'll pull me out of my ruminations to point out the snow on a cottonwood branch or watch a gopher snake slink through the meadows' edge. On summer nights, the stars call out our names.

Nashirah loves the summer horse shows. I do not. These shows began in my fourth year. At first, only small numbers of people came to watch us trot in a circle, jump, prance, and pull straw-filled wagons. Soon, more drove their cars and trucks into our valley. Boss had viewing stands built. The shows grew elaborate with seesaws, garlands, and a wild finale in which ranch hands and trainers, dressed as desert Arabs, rode us in an unruly stampede. Each time, the crowd jumped to its feet and cheered.

Nashirah is a horse show star. She has learned to bow to the audience and pretend to kiss the cowboys. She knows it is silly but still thinks it fine fun. I believe it is undignified. When I am forced to take part, while trotting in circles, false flowers around my neck, I imagine my next trail ride, a chance to drink from the creek and speak with the trees and, on return, listen as frogs and crickets sing to each other.

I am not bred. I do not prance for the public. It is fortunate, then, that I possess one trait that Boss values, one which allows me to stay. I am an excellent trail horse, especially good with reluctant riders.

While Boss likes to boast of his stud ranch, he also takes pride in showing off this land. Here in our valley of two creeks, ringed by mountains, Boss entertains his friends and also princes, diplomats, and men of immense wealth. Powerful men like to ride powerful horses, the tallest and finest-framed.

I am the horse he chooses for the hesitant ones who arrive with the commanding and influential. Boss tolerates these types. I welcome them. Men who listen more than speak. Cautious children. Wives and daughters who are in their own way corralled. Such people do not judge my stature or bearing, but instead look into my eyes. They look and then, boot in stirrup, climb onto my back.

As I take the trail, my confident stride assures them. I feel their hesitancy lose its grip. Steadily wending through spruce and pine forests, chipmunks skittering in the leaf litter, I embrace their rising joy. Gray jays and willow thickets accompany us on hillsides along cold, narrow creeks where alpine primrose grow. When we cross valleys filled with saffron gumweed and golden stonecrop, ten thousand tiny suns held by Mother Blue, my riders' own light shines.

It is here where our connection intensifies, a bodily communion born of more than proximity. It is here where my riders shout with praise or glee. Sometimes, children and women lean into my mane. As we exchange each other's scent, I remember my mother's words: Even as we are corralled, we are free.

The Grip
1965 & 2010

BECAUSE I AM seventy-one, the rangers offer to open the gate and drive me to the bunkhouse. "Hell, no," I tell them. "These legs work just fine."

No one laughs. Maybe I should have smiled when I said it. Maybe I should not have said it at all. Why couldn't I have simply been polite and replied, "I'll be sitting all day at tomorrow's symposium. A hike sounds divine."

Symposium. Is that different than a conference? Could we call it a panel discussion? Or is that mortifyingly dated? Hello, 1962.

Damn. My aging brain, spinning out of orbit. Again.

We are a full entourage this late September afternoon: two young Open Space rangers—male and female—that's nice to see, my symposium liaison Chloe, along with a second student filmmaker, a middle-aged administrator, and a local reporter.

I've never cared for reporters.

Even though everyone introduced themselves only minutes ago (except for Chloe who has been my contact since May), I can't remember a single name. Another hazard of advancing years.

Other than Chloe, who's Black, we are all white. After forty-five years in Los Angeles, this is striking. Aside from a family tearfully greeting a wife arriving home from Iraq, Chloe was the only Black woman I saw this morning in the airport's crowded welcome zone. Reminded me of my early days in production—me, the rare female in a sea of men. White men.

The group treats me like an aging Hollywood starlet, not the robust Colorado native who lurks under this wrinkled skin. No matter, I don't mind a little sycophancy. Or maybe, it's not about me at all. Maybe everyone is looking for an excuse to be outside, here in the mountain sunshine.

Should I tell them that the last time I was here, it rained for three days straight?

In the parking lot, the girl ranger hands me a bottle of Eldorado Springs water and I remember the Eldorado pool where we swam each summer, our June and August treat. Otherwise, it was the murky lake by my cousins' ranch. Which was fine for me, a country girl, broad-shouldered and strong.

We follow a trail that disappears into the trees. Nothing looks familiar, but the forest gives me time to collect my thoughts. How the symposium organizers found me, I'm still not sure. On the phone, Chloe had laughed at the question. "You can find anything on the web," she'd said.

"I was a grip on *Stagecoach*," I told her. "Are students interested in the technical end of movie making?" I wondered how much she knew about my life with Archie.

"Absolutely," she assured me. "Lighting, sound, wardrobe, directing, producing, writing—everyone gets a voice."

Turns out, I'm a celebrity. Local girl makes good, with a seat on two Women & Cinema panels, "The Other Side of the Camera: Women Pioneers," and "Collaboration is Key." While I am worlds away from Gillian Armstrong, Jane Campion, and Dawn Steel, God rest her soul, I have done my part. Although, to be sure, I've done it mostly shrouded. And yet, it's nice to be asked, to be acknowledged, and filming is nothing if not a team effort—

Oh, my whirling mind.

As the male ranger plucks a pine cone from a bed of groundcover, I see a badge on the pocket of his shirt and am relieved to have a second chance to remember his name. Oh. It's just a first initial and last name: Z. Jones.

Zeke? Zach? Zebulon? I have a grandson Zach.

Ranger Z. points out the difference between the pine cones of a Douglas fir and ponderosa pine while the girl ranger notifies me that aspen trees have natural sunscreen.

"Imagine that," I say.

They both talk about the history of the area, no longer called the Caribou Country Club Ranch but the more egalitarian, Caribou Ranch Open Space. They describe the silver mine, sound studio, and Arabian horse ranch which, at different times, all operated here. Meanwhile, I'm wondering, *Why don't I recognize anything?* The girl ranger—her shirt says *J. Holms*—moves to the front of our hiking group to chat with Chloe.

Early on in the symposium planning, someone did their math and discovered that 2010 was the 45th anniversary of the filming of Gordon's *Stagecoach*, here at the ranch. Then Chloe dug deeper and discovered that I, Annie Ames Archer, previously of Fort Lupton, Colorado, was part of Gordon's production crew.

Initially, I'd been lukewarm about flying to Colorado. My parents long gone and my brothers in Montana, I hadn't been to my home state in years. What caught my attention was Chloe's discussion of her proposed project, a movie adaptation based loosely on *Stagecoach*, with a Black cast and a Ford Huckster instead of a stagecoach. She plans to set it in the early 1920s when the Klan was on the rise in Colorado, substituting grand wizards and cross-burnings for "wild Indians." She'd been collaborating with two students in the Indigenous Studies program. "Everyone gets a place at the table," she'd told me.

"Or on the stagecoach," I'd added.

"Or in the Huckster," she'd quipped.

How I missed such repartee.

I listen now as Chloe describes her project to the ranger, then I say to her, "You've sharpened your elevator speech." She smiles because three months ago I hadn't heard the term. We'd called it a pitch or, in some crowds, a *schpiel*. Guess I've been out of the business too long.

It took three phone calls for me to understand that Chloe contacted me not simply because of my participation in *Stagecoach* and not only because I was Archie's wife (yes, *that* Archie), but because she knew, as others are now acknowledging, that after marrying Archie and leaving movie production (because that's what wives did back then), I became my husband's collaborator.

Those Best Original Screenplay Oscars and nominations for *Johnny Jones, 44 Oak Lane, The Steel Shoulder,* and the rest belonged as much to me as to Archie. He told me that himself. He said my behind-the-camera experience and my perspective as a member of the "female persuasion," as he put it, broke clichés and added vigor and appeal to his writing. *Vigor and appeal*—one of his favorite phrases.

He told me all that, but he didn't tell the world.

Maybe you wonder where that leaves me. What does one call the unpaid, untitled wife who was her husband's reviser, rewriter, and sounding board for thirty years? But hell, I did love it—our creative squabbles and breakthroughs, our partnership. At the time, wives didn't ask to be recognized. Did they?

As we walk through a sunny meadow dotted with golden-centered purple flowers, then back into wooded land, I let myself fall a step behind. I hear phrases floating out of context: *Legacy of Conquest. Lost Cause Movement. Center for the American West. Black Cowboy. Green Book. Limerick.* Limerick?

The long-ago teacher part of me wants to ask questions, but a bigger part is content to sip my water and breath this delicious air. Behind me, between crackles of the rangers' two-way radios, I hear talk of something called a barking beetle.

The reporter jogs toward me. "Miss Archer," he says, and I nearly stop him. It's either my professional name, Miss Ames, or my married name, Mrs. Archer, but not a mishmash of the two. I decide to behave and simply answer, "Yes?"

"What's your reply when people say Alex Cord was no John Wayne?"

He's talking about two actors who played Ringo Kid— John Wayne in Ford's 1939 original and Alex Cord, the man who stepped into Wayne's boots for the remake. *Our* remake. "And what people say that?" I ask, unsuccessfully masking my irritation.

The young man remains unfazed. "Well, was he?"

Certainly, you have a more original question than that, I want to say, but the University has flown me here, paid for my hotel room, and granted me a generous-enough stipend, so instead I tell him, "I thought it was a brilliant casting choice. Whereas John Wayne was portrayed as a cool outsider, Cord played a kinder, more human Ringo Kid. Consider how Ford and Gordon introduced them. Twirling a rifle against a blank sky versus sitting by a waterfall." The reporter scribbles. Does he not notice how rehearsed I sound? How I am stealing lines right and left from a *New York Times* reporter?

"Not to mention," I add, lowering my guard, "Alex was easy on the eyes." The scribbling intensifies and I see tomorrow's headline: *Local Girl Had Hots for Hollywood Star*. I snort. Quietly. Yes, Alex was a looker, but I hardly had time to watch.

Our group pauses at a fork in the trail, near an illuminated stand of aspens click-clattering in the breeze. The other film student asks me how I snagged the job on *Stagecoach*. I explain I was hired as an extra hand when a lighting grip was hit hard with altitude sickness.

"I always wondered what a grip was," Ranger Z. says. "You see that word all the time in movie credits."

"A grip is a technician," I say, then elucidate the roles of electric, lighting, and dolly grips. "My cousin's friend Henry was hired as a driver for Gordon Douglas— Gordon was the director," I add graciously, "and Henry heard they were looking for help and the next thing I know, I'm at the Harvest House Hotel in Boulder, standing in front of Harry Caplin, a business manager at 20th Century Fox, signing papers."

I put on a smile for the group. "One day, I'm on summer vacation, my first year of teaching eighth-graders just one month past, then boom!—I'm hauling cables, bolting cameras to dollies, and stacking apple boxes." I remember the film crew's uncertainty—who was this Wild West curiosity? After two days, they figured out I was not only strong, but that I paid attention and followed directions. That was good enough for them.

Turning right on the path, the rangers' conversation shifts to the Switzerland Trail railroad, on whose track bed we are now tromping along. My father once rode it once as a boy, his memories wistful.

My mind curves back further. What was this land like two hundred years ago? Three hundred? Three thousand? Were there man-made trails? Animal trails only, etched by deer and elk? Who stood at this vantage point and eyed the hills, shot a bow, threw a stone, embraced beneath an animal hide?

The vista widens and a red barn appears in the distance, its white roof the inverted V of a bird in flight. I wish I could say the entire shoot rushes back in, but filming is so much make-believe that there's an at-odds feeling between the work and the finished product. In short, it takes more than a location to jump start the memories.

Still, what a view.

We reach the bottom of the "lollipop," the part of the trail where the loop begins. Although in this case, as Ranger Z. has noted, the lollipop is shaped more like an amoeba. We continue west, bypassing the path to the ranch. We'll finish there, a small ceremony with local dignitaries, speeches, and, presumably, cake. But now our destination is the bunkhouse near the abandoned mine where we filmed the first stage coach stop. Did I remember that? No. I looked it up on IMDb. Chloe was right. You *can* find anything on the Internet.

As we walk, the reporter peppers me with questions. *Did Bing Crosby sing mid-shooting?* Not that I recall, but one of the grips said he heard him whistle and hum to himself. *Did the actors ride the horses or were there stuntmen?* Stuntmen, though, come to think of it, Slim did his own riding. He was a rodeo clown before becoming an actor.

Did all the stars sleep in one big tent in the valley? What a comical thought. Or is our budding reporter suggesting something lurid?

"We stayed in Denver," I tell him firmly, my tone edging toward schoolmarm. "Toward the end of the shoot, the stars stayed at the Harvest House. Make-up sessions began at 5:30 a.m."

Soon enough, we are walking single file along a path to the bunkhouse. I imagine they want me to gasp in recognition or break into a teary-eyed smile, but honestly, the weathered building reminds me of a dozen locations from a dozen films, some authentic like this, most not. After *Stagecoach*, I joined Gordon for his next film, the unmemorable *Chuka*, and what began as a two-week summer lark turned into a fifteen-year profession. Once *Chuka* wrapped, Jules got me on with Malpaso, Clint Eastwood's company, as they were filming *Hang 'Em High*. There, I met Archie.

Our intrepid crew sidles up to the long porch of the bunkhouse, where we drink more water and unwrap our energy bars. The reporter snaps photos and Ranger J. chats about the Blue Bird mine across the way. During the movie, the mine was hidden by a horse corral. I do remember that. I also remember the stack of firewood and the rain barrel which the set designers brought in to make the location look more authentic. As a first-time grip, all this had surprised me.

As we sit on the bunkhouse steps, the student film-maker who is not Chloe politely reintroduces herself as Tessa and asks, "When you were filming, did you feel as if you'd stepped back into the 1870's?" It's less of a bonehead question than the reporter's have been (his name, apparently, is Mark, as I just heard Chloe call him that) although it too speaks of a certain inexperience. Oh, what the hell. That's why I'm here. To educate.

"You have to remember, we don't shoot films in chronological order. To be economical, we schedule interior shots together, same with exterior ones, early morning shots, and so on. On Monday, for instance, we might shoot a scene where the leading lady and leading man are passionately kissing. On Tuesday? The scene where they first meet. It's hard to get lost in the story when it's that mixed up."

I shift on the century-old steps. *Is that a splinter in my backside?* "Remember, too, what you see on the screen is entirely different than what the crew experiences. Imagine an intimate moment between two actors on set. Then consider they are surrounded by cameramen, lighting technicians, sound recorders, animal wranglers, make-up artists, prop men. Of course, we add the stir-ring music later. And the sound—gun shots, hoof beats, pouring rain."

"So, it's just another job," Tessa says and I see I'm disappointing the lot of them. Best I don't tell them that the stagecoach itself was mounted on a truck trailer. Or that a horse was killed in a collision with a tree, right before filming.

Still, I've watched enough directors to know how to turn the conversation around. I stand, catch a whiff of pine bark in the dry air and something else. Is that water? I turn to the group, regaining my momentum. "When we do our job right," I say, "we transport *you* back to the 1870s." That earns me a smile. "I felt a small thrill each time I did my job well. Even when the scene required twenty takes."

I look across to the mine, uphill to a stone house that looks vaguely familiar, then back at Tessa. "There are stories within stories. For me, the story wasn't nine people riding a stagecoach. It was 150 people making a film—what happened before Gordon called *Action!* and after he yelled *Cut!* The moments I remember are helping Van Heflin take off his coat and zipping Ann Margaret's dress when the costumers had their hands full. That's what life is, stepping in where you're needed."

To myself, I wondered, Is that always true? When writing for Archie, had I stepped in too willingly?

Mark is writing in earnest and Tessa and Chloe are listening intently, so I shake off my second thoughts. "I felt pride as a woman working outside the industry's delegated roles. I was happy, as they say, to push that envelope." I was drawing from my prepared notes. Tomorrow, on stage, I'd have to make it sound fresh.

The administrator says, "I watched *Stagecoach* on video. I was wondering, did your crew fix up the inside of this bunkhouse to look like the boarding house or was that super-imposed?"

I pause before answering, realizing he must be a University, not County official, otherwise he'd know.

"We didn't film the interior shots here. Only the exteriors to take advantage of the... grand scenery and authentic buildings." He looks embarrassed, so I add. "But what a compliment to the film and editing crews for making it look so real." He smiles and I've dodged another bullet.

A radio crackles and Ranger Z. (Zeb? Zev? Zed-Zero-Zilch?) steps aside to talk. "What did you mean by apple box?" Ranger J. asks. "Did you help the lunch crew?"

"What?" Tessa asks.

"An apple box," Ranger J. repeats.

"You're a good listener," I tell her. "Apple boxes or half-apples, originally apple crates, are boxes for actors, mostly male actors to stand on. No actual apples involved. We use them to better fit the shot or simply to make the actors look taller. Sometimes they're called man-makers."

The girl—the *woman*—ranger, laughs. "And the difference between half and...?"

"Full? Full is eight inches, half is four, a quarter is two. A one-incher is called—"

"Apple sauce?"

This time, I laugh. I like a smart woman. "A pancake."

Ranger Z. steps back in. "Jim's sending two trucks to drive us back to the homestead."

Something occurs to me. "Is there a river there?" I ask, pointing beyond the bunkhouse and abandoned chicken coop.

"North Boulder Creek," Ranger Z. says. *Zeus? Zolton?*

"Can we look at it?" I ask. "For a minute."

Ranger J. exchanges glances with Ranger Z., then shoulders her day pack. Half the group stays put, testing their cell phones for reception, circling the bunkhouse in search of historic detritus. But Chloe, Ranger J. and I, and, of course, Mark, walk the short uphill to the river. The *creek*, not the *river*. I've become such an Angelino.

The water runs strong, white and dark blue, riffling over piles of rocks and half-submerged tree trunks. Chloe points out the remains of a train trestle, the spot where the railroad tracks crossed. I sit at the thoughtfully-provided picnic table, stare at the creek, and let it dislodge old thoughts. Ranger J. sits next to me. "Special memory?" she asks.

"I first met Jules here. We were both looking for a moment of solitude."

"Jules—your husband?" Mark asks.

"Archie Archer was her husband," Chloe corrects him.

"Paramour?" the ranger offers.

"Oh, no. Jules wasn't interested in... ah, girls."

"He was gay?" This from Chloe, as much of a statement as a question. I forget how routine homosexuality is for this generation. How unhesitant they are.

"Cool," Mark says. Scribble. Scribble.

"Jules was the gaffer for *Stagecoach*. Head of lighting." I stare into the forest. "Jules loved the early and late day sun." I turn to Chloe. "We worked together on two more films and then he introduced me to Archie. Jules and I... We've been friends for forty-four years." Does a friendship end when one of you dies?

"Jules passed away last year," I clarify. "Archie, four years ago. I miss them both very much."

"I'm sorry," Ranger J. says. She puts her hand on my shoulder.

"Thank you, dear," I say, feeling ninety instead of seventy-one. "Tell me your name again."

Kindly, she doesn't roll her eyes. "Julia," she says.

"No kidding?"

"No kidding."

I shake my head at the playfulness of the gods, then point. "Look at the light on the water." Chloe, Julia, and I watch the sunlight hopscotch on the creek's surface. Mark puts down his notebook and watches too.

Our moment ends with the sound of a truck engine. "It's the cavalry," Julia intones with the regret of someone who loves nature more than people.

As Chloe and Mark hop into the truck bed, Ranger Z. gives me a hand climbing into the passenger seat. He tosses Julia the keys before joining the others in back. "Zander hates to drive," Julia confides. *Zander!* I never would have guessed.

K-turning on the dirt incline, Julia heads back to the road. "Tell me something," she says. "Which actors stood on an apple box?"

I raise an eyebrow. "I'm a professional. I'll never tell."

She nods. "Good on you."

In a ridiculously short time, we pass the bunkhouse, drive onto the "lollipop," turn left toward the homestead, and, voila! we are sitting on folding chairs facing its porch. Faculty from the film department have joined us, along with the Open Space director, a County

67

commissioner, and a dozen volunteers. I smile and shake hands and cut a sheet cake that reads, in Wild West lettering, STAGECOACH. Below that, a piped-icing drawing of a canvas-covered chuckwagon. It's the wrong kind of wagon, the kind where tourists eat bowls of chili in dude ranch campgrounds, but I appreciate the effort. Below the wagon, *Annie Ames Archer*. I appreciate that too.

When I'm asked to speak about *Stagecoach*, I take the mike, recoil at the feedback, and retell the story of how I was hired. I describe non-linear film making and the days of rain that caused the final shootout scene to be filmed elsewhere. My audience seems eager for more, so I tell them what I learned that summer and the years after—that actors are human and humans are unpredictable. They swear when they foul up. Or they laugh. They snap at each other. They comfort each other. They are wildly different off set than they are on. Or they are exactly the same.

This is the point where I'm supposed to introduce Chloe, but as I look beyond the audience into the meadow, I think of Jules. Yes, he was vibrant, funny and well-loved. Yes, he lived a rich life. But how much of that life, how much of *himself,* had to be lived on the sly? Early on, he'd smile when I showed concern, pat my shoulder, say how living in the shadows was glamourous, romantic even.

Funny thing for a gaffer to say.

I think of the symposium panel "Collaboration is Key." I'd rolled my eyes when I'd first read it, but now, in this wide, high altitude meadow, I interrogate myself.

Why *hadn't* I done more? In those years of deep closets, those years of plague, Archie and I could have done far more. Out of the shadows and into the public glare.

What can I do now?

I take a deep breath of this thin, brilliant air. "Standing here," I say, "remembering that summer, remembering this place, I find myself *forgetting*. Or rather, thinking about forgetting. How I've forgotten so many of the sets I've worked on, crews I've work with, hell, even most of your names shortly after we'd been introduced." A purr of polite, forgiving laughter.

"But looking at this land," I continue, "I'm aware of another kind of forgetting. The convenient kind. Forty-five years ago, we filmed gunfights and 'massacres' in this valley, bedecking a cast of extras as Indians, as Sioux, with Hollywood feathers and Hollywood paint. We, and by we, I mean the film studios, were part of a long tradition of—" I search for the right word in this impromptu blast of words, "of *demonizing* native peoples. We contributed to prejudice and violence far beyond the movie screen."

I take a breath. "I know that's changed some, with deeper characterizations, but also with different stereotypes. The wise Indian. The noble... the spiritual..." I stare at my audience, most sitting, some standing, some shifting. They'll allow me some leeway. Or not. Either way, I stumble ahead.

"I wanted to acknowledge that and apologize for my part in it." I hesitate. "Apologies don't make for much, though. But action...." I remember something I saw on the internet, companies with funny names, Indiegogo and... Kickstand? No, Kick*starter*. Fundraising websites. An idea sprouts in my mind.

"*Stagecoach* has been made and remade three times now—it's a powerful story. But always on a biased slant. Chloe Daniels, who you all can thank for getting me off my California keister to fly on out here"—this draws murmured laughter for which I am thankful—"has a vision for carrying on the legacy of *Stagecoach* through one of the most fascinating reinterpretations yet.

"Now, visions are where ideas incubate, but in our harsh reality, movies need... money." I was wildly off script, but, I realized, having more fun than I'd had in months. Years. "Money," I repeated. "Movies need it and that's why I am starting a fundraiser for Chloe's film, *Huckster*. I'll now let Chloe tell you all about it."

Facing me, Chloe accepts the mike with a perplexed expression, but she's all aplomb when she turns to her audience. "Time for the elevator speech," I whisper.

I walk to the edge of the audience and listen to Chloe. As she speaks, the past drifts in. Horses whinnying in their stalls. Red Buttons cracking a joke. I smell fresh hay tossed over a fence and the scent of Vitalis in Mike Connors' hair. I feel Jules' hand on my shoulder as he says, "Will you look at that sunset? Those shadows? That light?"

The Sound Master

1977

THE SMALL FLAME materialized, vanished, appeared again. Shallow breathing, then a quick, "Dammit."

From the darkness, Russell asked, "Bow?"

The flame blinked out. "Holy crap, Russell! You scared me."

"Me?" Russell asked, amused. "You're the one sneaking through the trees, flicking your Bic."

Bow. Short for Elbow. A variation on Elbert. Shaggy-haired, the new roadie for Flight Pattern reminded Russell of a wind-up chicken, pecking and hopping, pecking and hopping. Bow was everywhere at once: hauling equipment, hooking up mikes, hooking up amps, collecting the dead soldier beer bottles that amassed by the hour. Reliable for sure, no argument there, but Bow never stopped chattering. He never mellowed the hell out.

Bo lowered his lighter. "Jesus, man, we coulda lost you. It's dark out here. Double damn dark."

"There's a moon," Russell observed. "Nearly full."

"Me and the boys thought you went off for a leak and got eaten by a wolf." Bow stretched his neck toward the valley below, as if he might see one right now.

After twelve hours in the recording studio, Russell wanted to be alone, free from human voices and electric bass. "No wolves around here," he mused. "All shot out years ago." He tried to be patient, to dissuade Bow with a minor key rather than a major one. They did, after all, have to work together, all of them pretty much on top of each other, for the next six days.

"Then a leopard," Bow offered. "Or a cheetah."

Russell laughed despite his impatience. He had been damn lucky to get this gig, the chance to work the console at the famed—no, the *fabled*—Caribou Ranch recording studio. In L.A., he mostly worked with up-and-coming bands that dropped him if they got big. Occasionally, he engineered Christmas albums for solo artists wanting to pull in extra cash, although his preference was for still-talented acts whose day in the spotlight was over.

Russell thought his own chance for glory had passed until Flight Pattern's fourth album, *Boxing Ring*, turned gold. Brought on early by manager Kit Kimble, Russell had engineered the band's first three releases. "Respectable efforts" and "Serious potential," reviewers had expounded in *Rolling Stone* and *Spin*.

Then, last summer, Flight Pattern had hit it big with two 45s: "Roughshod Boy" and "Dig Down Deep," which charted at #1 and #4. After *Boxing Ring* was released, bass guitarist and vocalist Ron Bellow's unassuming

"Sunday Dinner (without Jim)" was embraced as an anti-war ballad, winning considerable air time during the weeks before Christmas.

Critics now described Flight Pattern as *overlooked, unappreciated* and, *"The best band you've never heard of,"* comparing it to Chicago, The Nitty Gritty Dirt Band, and The Eagles, now that Joe Walsh had joined them.

It was a lot to live up to.

Kit Kimble decided to soothe collective jitters by celebrating Flight Pattern's success. He announced he wanted to "solidify the band," a euphemism, Russell knew, for addressing rumors that Ron Bellow and Even Steven, the group's percussionist, were toying with the idea of starting their own group.

When a ten-day slot opened at Caribou (the lead guitarist of an undisclosed band had fractured his arm in a motorcycle accident), Kit had grabbed the spot. The astounding luck for Russell was that Caribou's studio engineer, hearing about the fractured arm, had booked himself a week in Barbados.

Which is why, three days ago, Russell found himself running his fingers over the Neve console, assuring himself that this mile-high fairytale was real. And, why, right now, Russell was standing on a chilly hillside, musing over the setting moon.

"Hey Russ," Bow said, "did you hear that Kit might change the album name to *Thin Air*? Like Elton John did with *Caribou*? But *Thin Air* is better because it's two things: thin air like *vanishing into* and thin air, because, well, the air here *is* thin."

When Russell didn't reply, Bow continued. "Did you know that when John was here—John freakin' Lennon!—he drove into Nederland and bought himself a pair of cowboy boots? Goddamn cowboy boots! And, nobody—get this—*nobody* blinked an eye."

"Huh."

"Why wouldn't Russell talk to him?" Bow wondered. One last stab with the wonky engineer, he decided.

"What are you doing out here?"

"Looking at the moon."

Russell envisioned the wood-paneled studio, with its here-and-there clatter of folding chairs, over-filled ashtrays, and tottering mike stands, weirdly evocative of tall, starving penguins. Next, he brought to mind the instruments which filled the studio—guitars (steel, bass and acoustic), drums and snares, horns and keyboards, the nickel-plated sleigh bells. Finally, he pictured the men who filled the space—the unshaven, perspiring, beer-breathed, nicotine-drenched men—then imagined it all, *them* all, evaporating into the ether, effortlessly replaced by this soft-white, three-quarter moon.

"The moon?" Bow repeated, voice cracking. "Damn, son. You're always looking at the moon." Bow liked to call Russell *son* even though Russell was twelve, maybe fifteen, years older. "Same moon as last night. Doesn't blink. Doesn't change colors. Just a chunk of rock in sky."

Russell narrowed his eyes. "The moon, our view of it, is always changing. You know that." Bow did know it, didn't he? "Full moon? Half moon? Crescent moon?"

"What's that?" Bow said, distracted. He took a drink of beer, tilted the bottle toward Russell. "Want a swig? It's a Coors."

"No. Thanks, though."

Bow finished the bottle. "Gawd, I miss Sunset Strip. I miss streetlights, headlights, even traffic lights." He lit a cigarette. "I could use a night at the Whiskey or even the Troubadour. Any noisy bar with stale pretzels and a sticky floor. Hell, I could use a bar fight."

Russell shook his head. Wasn't the point of being here to get away from all that? The reason for clearing the calendar, corralling the equipment, triple-checking you hadn't left anything—cables, headphones, sheet music—and piling into the bus for a too-long ride, all so that you could embrace this expansive, crisp-aired, world on-high?

Bow lit his lighter and checked his watch. "Son, it's late. Or early. You coming back with us? One Jeep's still there."

"In a little while."

Today's session had wrapped long after midnight. The still-buzzed, still-energized band had commandeered two Jeeps and driven the dirt road west, pulling over—or rather, parking right on the road, since Guercio owned the whole crazy four thousand acres here—to light up, drink down, and howl away their strung-out exhaustion.

Only Russell had wanted to cool his jets.

Bow ground his latest cigarette on the sole of his new boot. "They won't wait much longer. You don't want to *walk* back."

"I've walked back before," Russell said.

Bow lit another cigarette, took two puffs, then stared at it as if it had materialized of its own volition. He tapped it out and slipped it back in the pack. "What a day, huh? Didn't think the Big Guy was gonna find his way on that last one, did you? Then he put pedal to the metal and jammed it out. Jammed it, sir!"

Big Guy. Why couldn't Bow call the lead guitarist Terry, like everyone else?

Bow fidgeted, but something kept him from walking. "You're a puzzle, Russell Rayback. Our crew-cut, battle-scarred, scary-intense sound engineer. Our," Bow paused for effect, "Sound Master!"

Nothing.

Bow reached back into the pack for his half cigarette and pulled out another, offering it. "Coffin nail?"

"I don't smoke."

"You don't smoke. You don't drink. You don't snort. You haven't made friends with a single Caribouette. What *do* you do?"

"I listen."

"In there, sure," Bow cocked his thumb in the direction of the studio, "but here? What's there to listen to out here?"

"Plenty," Russell answered, "when you stop talking."

Bow snorted, but tried listening. For about fifteen seconds. "Nope. Nada. Sorry." He rubbed his hands together. "Never thought I'd be hankering for the sound of screeching brakes, the sound of a drunk cursing the bouncer who's thrown him out of the Roxy. This place, I know it's America the Beautiful and all, but it's so damn quiet. It's spooky."

"You work for a band, for bloody sake," Russell snapped, patience finally gone. "You *have* to know how to *listen*." He stared Bow down. "Listen up, Elbow Jones—close your eyes and tell me what you *hear*."

Bow concentrated. "Buzzing. I guess I hear buzzing."

"Buzzing?"

"Well, like a broken buzzing. A dot dot dash sound."

"Those are crickets. Good. What else?"

"You know, Russell, I need to pee."

"Listen!"

Bow pushed his eyes shut. "A plane. Maybe?"

Russell could fill the fingers of his left hand with everything *he* was hearing. The crickets. Bow's boots snapping twigs underfoot. A breeze entertaining the aspen leaves. Earlier, the *ooo-ooo* of an owl. A bird, or snake, rustling in the brush. Were snakes nocturnal? He had known that once, when he was nine.

"Wait, what was that?" Bow asked.

"Which one?"

"That zig-zaggy sound. Squeaky."

"Chorus frogs. There's a pond in the valley."

"How do you know that?"

"I've gone walking. I've seen it."

"When?"

"First morning. When you all were sleeping off your hangovers."

"Huh. Look, I really gotta drain the lizard. Be right back."

When Bow returned, zipping his jeans, he heard a low hum emanating from Russell. "Now what?"

"What if we combined them somehow? As a kid, I heard them on my dad's tiki bar lounge records, but that was trumped-up stuff, squawking parrots and overdubs of roaring surf. Felt more like a gag than true…"

"Whoa, son. Start at the beginning."

"What if we took the equipment out here and recorded the crickets and coyotes. The rattling aspen and chorus frogs."

"Like, for science class?"

"For the beauty of it. Add in flute, cello, or that thing that Harrison plays—a dobro. Long notes. Wide spaces. Time to think."

"Think about what?"

"And some Indian music. American Indian." It was as if Russell were in a trance. He turned to Bow. "Was it the Utes who lived here? The Cheyenne? Never mind. I'll ask Sammie Begaye. You know him?"

"Sammy in L.A. who plays the trombone?" Bow asked. "He's Navajo." Bow paused. "Sorry, I still don't get it. This whole at-one-with-nature thing."

Russell looked at his unwanted companion. "At some point, Bow, we're going to outgrow the drinking and drugs and sex and all-nighters—"

Bow thrust out his hand like a traffic cop. "Slow down, cowboy. I ain't outgrowing nothing. Hell, I'm still growing into it." He tugged on his jacket. "I know this profession is about listening and the band is about 'the sound,' but for me, it's also about, hell, it's *all* about, helping make that happen. The fights, the shouting, the frustration when nothing is going right or one thing, the same thing, over and over, isn't going right, riding that out until the moment when it cracks open and everything falls together, flies together, not just the notes, pitch, or timing, but the all. When Ron nails it and grins like a kid and the Big Guy grins back, or when Even Steven loses himself in a riff or Leo plays the Gilligan's Island song and everyone cracks up. That's why I'm here."

In the darkness, Russell smiled.

"It's about the warm-ups, the goof-ups, the experiments that don't go anywhere but are beautiful anyway. I know I'm only a roadie, but nobody but us is ever going to hear that. That's something, man."

"That's a lot," Russell acknowledged. He nearly added, *Maybe I am missing something,* but even as he thought it, he knew he'd never been a "one-of-the-gang" boy and he'd never be a "one-of-the-boys" man. He stood apart. That's what made Russell good at his job. That's what made him, him.

"Bow," Russell asked, "want to walk back to the Jeep?"

As they hiked the ridge, Russell blended synthesizer and lighting storm in his head. Harp and bird song.

"Hey, Russell," Bow said, "when Billy Joel was here, he didn't stay in his own cabin, but hung with his band in the lodge. He's that cool. And Joe Walsh—he was the first—and the bathrooms weren't finished, so he peed in the horse stalls. True story."

"That so?" Russell said. Spring creek. Oboe. Inter-weaving.

The Jeep was gone but dawn was nearing. Early birds, real ones, sung from the branches.

The Ranger
2008

WINTER AT CARIBOU. The absence of the trail trans-
figures the forest. For a moment, no prescribed way
forward until the diamond blazes reorient me. I walk,
certain this new snow has pushed wider the space
between trunks.

I remember what Donald Peattie wrote: "Winter is a
study in halftones, and one must have an eye for them,
or go lonely." After July's carnival of wildflowers, after
the rush of incandescent aspen leaves, the land is ready
for muted reflection. Brown-grey bark. Dark green
needles. Pale grasses.

As I walk, I keep an eye out—what ranger doesn't?—
yet I also study the dearth of leaves, flowers, trails, and
color. Absence is revelation. The shape of the land—its
swells and slopes. Slender aspen branches, free from
leaves. One white hillside, striped by a thousand tree
trunk shadows.

As I near the meadow, I'm aware of a quiet rebellion. Not all is monotone after all. A blue cast to the snow. The burgundy branch of the low-lying willow. Even the aspen bark is a pale mint green—chlorophyll, silently photosynthesizing. And these juniper berries, a protest in periwinkle and dusky blue.

I never go lonely here.

My trained self looks for damaged fences, trampled shrubs, trails that shouldn't be trails, people who shouldn't be where they are. Today though, this early midweek morning, humans are few. There's time to watch and listen and to decipher prints in the snow. Coyote. Fox. Bobcat? Paws wide or narrow? Claws visible? The invisible ones, watching me.

Conifers. My steady, visible, companions. Doug firs and ponderosa pines lining the way. Engelmann spruce on the hillside. A Colorado blue spruce, *Picea pungens,* rises, sentinel, beyond the willow carr. How many shades of green can that stately tree claim? Near the steps to the creek, a friendly limber pine. I shake its hand.

North Boulder Creek, always off trail, never claiming attention. The heart of my winter trek. Snow, dolloped like frosting, tops the creek's boulders. Icy lace collars them. Translucent and brittle, the ice gives way in sunlight, reforms at night.

Below, air bubbles—dark amoeba shapes—joggle by. They stretch and shrink, pause and regroup, accompanied by a deep percussion of gulps, gurgles and plunks. I listen until I am thoroughly chilled, until my body calls for motion and sunlight.

I pull my cap over my ears and climb the steps to the trail, red-berried kinnikinnick trimming its edges, the babble and bounce of the creek still in my ears.

As I circle out of the trees onto the wide trail, other sounds ride the wind—guitar riffs, train whistles, horses trotting, willow branches snapping, an ore cart spilling its load. I think of what this land has been and what it might have become. A country club? A golf course? Six sprawling mansions?

I think about who we first stole this land from and who we stole it from after that. What would it feel like to have centuries upon centuries of connection to a place? To be forced from it?

This side of winter solstice, the days are lengthening. In a few months, the air will warm, the snow will melt, the rains will come. Sap will run. Buds will swell and burst and blossom. Leaves uncurl, petals unfurl, elks calve, and birds perch. Thunderheads will dominate the sky and visitors will fill the trails. Days will pass and petals fade. Green will go gold. Both will drop. Darkness gathering sooner, staying longer.

Snow will fall again.

This is the cycle we're given, a world that oscillates between subtle and striking.

The light on the hillside has shifted. The shadow stripes are gone. I close the loop and head for home.

The Writer

2015

THE WRITER HAS been here before. Early summers, early fall, a winter snowshoe once. This, though, is something new: the leisure of morning and late afternoon, the wonder of darkness. Now there's no hustling to the parking lot before twilight encroaches. No rushed drive up the canyon from home. Home is here.

The writer as audience. In this open-air theater of changing sky, she applauds sunset, moonrise, daybreak, and the Milky Way. At night, she tucks herself into the lower bunk in the pine-paneled cabin, abandoned horse stalls on the other side of the wall—a wall that divides her cozy room from old straw and earth floor, this century from the last.

She carries her breakfast to the picnic table. The ground squirrels scatter. The family of swallows rush out, circle, and return to their mud nest over the outdoor sink. A mug of tea. A book of poems. Paper. Maps.

She sits. She listens. She adds a line of words to her composition book. A note to her journal. She examines the maps, compares the printed paper to the real thing. She watches shadows shift, feels the air warm. She reads Robert Sund and writes about a child on a train. She admires the sky. How can you not admire the sky? Each bird, breeze, flower, and cloud is a distraction. Each bird, breeze, flower and cloud is why she is here.

She hopes to see a moose.

She faces south at the picnic table. Looks east, looks west. Far pond, farm house, pebbled road, aspen grove, hay field. Mountains. Mountains. Mountains. In this expanse, horses once cantered, dogs herded, Herefords grazed, brown-backed, white-faced. They are all long gone. They are all right here.

She considers her day, the one before and the one to be. This is her favorite part, this early morning mulling. The possibilities here in the heart of the heart of this valley.

These words keep surfacing: *Savor. Astonishment. Delight.*

Human history fills this land, but this morning, the natural world fills her. (When did we start separating the two?) Yellow stonecrop. Golden banner. One-sided penstemon. Northern bed-straw. Mountain harebell.

Mountain bluebird. Two Abert's squirrels, on a flat rock, among the aspens. A cloud tower in the eastern sky. *Cumulonimbus.*

She logs where she has walked. Private trail over North Boulder Creek. Private trail west along Delonde Creek. (The perks of a residency!) Behind the homestead. Around the bunkhouse. Round and round the loop.

She logs where she has sat. Beside the train trestle. Beside the pond. Beside the creek, to the east and north. On a small wooden bridge, no one else in sight. And when: Under a generous sun. In a drizzle. At dusk.

She still hasn't seen a moose.

A ranger told her: You don't look for moose. You listen for them. The sploosh, sploosh of their hooves in marsh land.

She learns the arc of the sun. She photographs pink-trimmed evening clouds. *Stratocumulus.* She watches the translucent moon through her spotting scope. She stands under a sea of stars. Once people believed stars to be tears in the fabric of the sky, portholes between this world and the next. She imagines the beyond and feels it inside her, no veils at all.

On her last full day, she wakes early and walks to the pond. Robins perch, flickers dart, bluebirds dot the fence posts. Dark patches spot the trail. Drying dew or something else? She looks up from the damp dashed line to see a long face, tall legs between the aspen trunks and shrub thicket. She edges left, staying on her side of the fence. Sits and watches and watches.

The next morning, she drives out of the valley. Around the red barn, down the red dirt road. She drives reluctantly until she sees them waiting for her. Cow and bull and calf. Fur and hoof and antlers. Moose send-off party. Musky marsh farewell.

Author's Note

CARIBOU RANCH OPEN SPACE lies within Boulder County, the ancestral homeland and unceded territory of many peoples for many millennia.

These peoples and nations include the Di De'i (Apache), Hinono'eiteen (Arapaho), Tsistsistas (Cheyenne), Nʉmʉnʉʉ (Comanche), Kiowa, Čariks i Čariks (Pawnee), Sosonih (Shoshone), Oc'eti S'akowin (Sioux) and Núuchiu (Ute).

From 1862 to 1865, John Evans served as governor of the then territory of Colorado. Following decades of brutal treatment of native peoples, in 1864, the U.S. Cavalry, under the direction of Evans, deliberately attacked a peaceful village of forcibly relocated Cheyenne and Arapaho people living near Sand Creek in eastern Colorado. Soldiers slaughtered approximately 230 people, mostly infants, women, and elders, including Chief Left Hand (Niwot/Nawath), a diplomat and linguist, and the leader of the last Hinóno'éí band to spend their winters in the Boulder Valley.

The U.S. government forced survivors of the massacre out of Colorado to reservations in Wyoming and Oklahoma, where most Hinóno'éí live today.

. . .

The University of Colorado at Boulder houses the Center for Native American and Indigenous Studies. The center provides Native students, staff, and faculty an intellectual and social home. It promotes collaborative research and encourages conversations. Learn more about the Center and donate to support its work at colorado.edu/cnais.

. . .

This book's first chapter, "The Storyteller," tells of mice finding shelter in a "green-fingered" tree. This tree, *Pseudotsuga menziesii*, is often called a Douglas Fir. Its distinctive female seed cones do feature mice-like feet and tail protrusions.

Angelica Lawson, Ph.D., professor at the University of Colorado at Boulder, notes that the story of the mice is a "somewhat generic" Indigenous tale, most often set in the Pacific Northwest. Coast Douglas firs grow there, while Rocky Mountain Douglas firs grow here in Colorado.

Professor Lawson further explains that in different accounts of the story, the mice are escaping a hawk, a fox, or a fire. In other scenarios, the generous Douglas Fir offers its seeds to one hungry mouse, whose fellow mice eventually overwhelm the tree, causing the Douglas fir to trap the mice within its cones.

Oddly, the Douglas fir (named for Scottish botanist David Douglas, and sometimes called an Oregon pine or Douglas spruce), is neither a fir, pine, or spruce. Referring to its taxonomic confusion, its scientific genus name *Pseudotsuga* means "false hemlock."

Acknowledgments

I AM GRATEFUL to everyone who helped me make the most of my 2015 residency at Caribou Ranch.

Boulder County's Larry Colbenson introduced me to Caribou during a volunteer training two decades ago. Pascale Fried and Rebekah Bloyd encouraged me to re-apply for this residency even as competition for it grew fierce. Lori Fuller, Martha Coder, and Berit Naeseth visited during my stay, adding their observations and sense of adventure.

Dylan Yates opened her home to a new writing group at which many of these stories took their initial shape. Wendy Hall and Marti Anderson of Boulder's Carnegie Branch Library suggested books and unearthed audio recordings, photographs, and decades-old newspaper clippings for me. Sheryl Kippen, Boulder County's Cultural History Program Coordinator for Parks and Open Space, provided information about mining and tourism at Bluebird. Michael O'Neill graciously shared his expertise of the Switzerland Trail railroad. Ilo

Orleans was instrumental on matters of film production for "The Grip" while Amy Gup's mention of telepathic horses influenced "The Trail Rider."

Author and educator Jason Evans offered excellent feedback and insights on writing authentic African-American characters. Valuable critiques from Dr. Angelica Lawson, Professor of Film Studies and Ethnic Studies at the University of Colorado/Boulder, improved my representation of Indigenous characters and culture, and helped inform my revisions of "The Storyteller," "The Artist," and "The Grip."

Much appreciation to editor Juan Morales at Colorado State University/Pueblo for publishing "The Cook's Son" in *Pilgrimage Magazine*.

Thanks too, to Martha Coder and Magic Morningstar for taking author photos, and to Sue Trainor, Alison Conte, Diane Denenberg, and Rebekah Bloyd for feedback and proofreading. I take full responsibility for all remaining errors, as I am an endless reviser. Diane also offered botanical know-how during a winter hike at Caribou, inspiring material for "The Ranger."

Sarah Andrews, Caribou's real resident ranger, was instrumental during my stay, offering advice on hiking trails, moose sightings, and solar showers.

Finally, gratitude to all the creatures, creeks, and wildflowers of Caribou. You bring me joy with every visit.

Photo by Martha Coder

Author, assemblage artist, and waterfall enthusiast, ELLEN ORLEANS has written *Inside, The World Is Orange*, a memoir; *Outreach*, a prize-winning chapbook from Gertrude Press; and five books of queer humor, including Lammy winner *The Butches of Madison County*.

Ellen's stories have appeared on NPR's *Hanukkah Lights* and have been performed by Denver's Buntport Theater and Hangar Theatre in New York. Her work has been published in *Primal Picnics*, *Women's Glib*, *A Poetic Inventory of Rocky Mountain National Park*, *The Washington Post*, *The Denver Quarterly*, *Palimpsest*, *Pilgrimage*, *Girljock*, *Lost Paper*, and many more.

Ellen has taught writing in schools, libraries, and along hiking trails. She also leads story hikes for toddlers and manages sustainability programs for the City of Boulder. Write to her at orleanswriting@gmail.com.